THE END

THE NEW BEGINNING

Acknowledgments

A GREAT BIG THANKS:

to (Agent Cookie) Mariann Mcbride-Parks for seeing in me, the ability to write a good story and the encouragement to see it through to the end.

to my cousin Ila Foster for planting the seed a few years ago, which made me receptive to Mariann's request.

to Yvonne Venables for so generously donating hours of her time to proof read and edit the book.

to Dr. Jane L. Cameron for listening to the story-line and prompting me to write more.

to Robert at Theophania Publishing for publishing my story.

Cover designed by author using a photograph of the western sunset.

Phototography by Becci Featherstone.

Sincerely,
Jo-Anne Foster

INDEX

SECTION ONE

THE END

Chapter:

SECTION TWO

THE NEW BEGINNING

Chapter:

INDEX CONTINUED

SECTION TWO

THE NEW BEGINNING

Chapter:

Section One

THE END

Chapter One

Something is Astir

I'm a late sleeper. I begin my day close to noon when the sun is shining. If I get up when the rays have burned clouds and fog away I have a chance of cheeriness.

Well, that was not going to happen today. The sun was shining all right but I felt unsettled. I stepped out onto the balcony with a steaming cup of coffee hoping to revive myself, but the air felt rather odd. I looked east, west, all around (after all, all odd feelings must be the fault of the weather). No, nothing unusual there, so what was the problem? "I have to quit watching those murder mysteries late at night. It's my imagination!"

I immediately set my coffee down, made my way swiftly to the car and drove up the hill to the market. Ah yes, I felt much better there among the produce. Nothing like vegetable therapy! I hadn't eaten apricots in ages and they smelled delicious. I wanted some cold cuts too. The owners of this small store roasted their own meat daily and sliced it to the perfect thickness. They had the best quality of everything.I looked to my right. There was a tall man, slim, with slightly wavy dark hair and warm brown eyes looking back. I was not interested in a relationship but it didn't hurt to admire someone else's catch. He commented on the fresh produce and I remarked "This particular market is always exceptional." That sounded boring. Whatever, there's no need to impress anyone.

We began some small talk, but according to my heart racing, he must have been saying something rather exciting. "I'm not that foolish." I told myself, "It's the unsettled feeling creeping into my mind again." Gradually, we got into the rhythm of a mutually enjoyable conversation and things went much better from there.

As we stood at the check-out, he introduced a new turn on the topics; something more personal. He said he was there from the States to visit his brother who lived a couple of blocks away. His brother, Ty, ran a business from his home and worked very long hours with clients back-to-back. With demanding hours, he did not eat properly. He went for a run every morning and night, and had an awesome gym on the lower floor but ate out of the fridge – whatever was handy. I snickered "A lot of single people eat that way."

We paid for our groceries then the tall stranger invited me to accompany him to the coffee shop a few doors down. We chose seats on the patio in the sun. He introduced himself "Richard".

He said, "I have a reason for talking to you. I've been asking around the neighborhood for someone who has the time to make simple food such as sandwiches, and perhaps a fruit smoothie, to serve Ty between clients; also a stew or casserole that keeps well in the oven, to help himself to at the end of the day. However, it seems that everyone in this neighborhood has a career, children, then in the evening work out at a spa. I have to leave in a couple of days and I've had no success." I noted that he was very easy to talk to and had excellent communication skills. He looked at me when he was speaking, not all around to see what everyone else was doing. There are few good communicators.

He went on to explain, "Each client is with him from three or four, to sometimes six hours. They do not need to be greeted. They come at an agreed time, and go straight into his office through the front entrance. There is a professional coffee machine which is maintained regularly, avoiding the need for fresh beverages to be served in the office. They help themselves; the machine gives them a fresh brewed cup of coffee each time."

I revealed "I have the time, perhaps, but I like it for myself. I wouldn't mind helping out a little, I guess, but it sounds rather time consuming. It may sound selfish but that's just the way I prefer to live."

"Could we make a compromise?" Richard asked. "He would require his first sandwich

9

around ten in the morning. You could leave about three more sandwiches in the fridge, then come back sometime in the evening to make the casserole. He eats dinner anywhere from ten to midnight; like I said, long working hours."

"What does he like in his smoothies?" I inquired. "You're an angel", he replied with a twinkle in his eyes. He took a sip of his coffee and in a softer tone "If you wouldn't mind, it would be necessary to pick up your day's supplies here, at this store, on your way to his house. I have already spoken to the store manager about allowing credit that will be paid monthly. You are welcome to make sandwiches for yourself, as well as extra dinner that you can take home with you. Does that sweeten the pot?" We shared a smile of mutual understanding.

He then did a rather odd thing. He looked around at the sky in all directions. He then asked if I felt something unusual in the atmosphere. My mouth fell open. I told him I was hesitant to say anything but I had felt it from the time I got up. It was one reason I came up to the market, hoping to shake the feeling. I told him I was amazed he felt it too. "What does it feel like to you?" I inquired, very anxious to hear his reply.

He took his time, considered his answer, and replied "Something is astir."

Chapter Two

Ty

"Will you take a walk down the street with me to the house and meet Ty? He's through early today and has time for a conversation. Meeting him will probably help you make a decision." I agreed with him.

Along the way, we talked a little about Ty and the family. They come from a family of ten boys. Their mother left shortly after the birth of the last child. She went to live in Boston with her sister. She and their father were no longer happy in their relationship, and she didn't want to be tied to raising ten boys. She felt that she was domestic help, and nothing more. "I understand her" he said, "Papa's a very good business man but a bad husband. He runs the ranch, and supervises several family businesses."

He ordered more coffee, then continued, "Each son, as well as performing duties on the ranch, has his own separate business which our Papa co-ordinates from his office. Papa does all the paperwork with the help of one accountant. He's not good in relationships but a master of his ship." He said all the boys seemed satisfied with the situation and respected their Papa as having a gift of generating success. In return for Papa's involvement, a certain amount of their income went into running the ranch itself.

Shifting the topic back to his brother, "Ty's the only one that doesn't thrive in that atmosphere. He's a lone wolf. He likes to run his own life and his own businesses. One's not enough to occupy his mind sufficiently – he runs several. He's a bit of a stray, but what a remarkable stray! Everything he puts his time into turns to gold. He's very definitely a genius on many different levels and has the disposition to go with it as well. I don't mean he's difficult, he's actually very pleasant to talk to but has the patience for only short conversations. He's always preoccupied. I understand him and love him dearly. He can't be bothered with grocery shopping or making meals. He doesn't like restaurants. He just needs food to be convenient for him. He will eat anything put before him, but you can ask him yourself. Here we are."

It was a beautiful house, outside and inside. I fell immediately in love with it and at home in the surroundings. Richard invited me to sit on a stool at the counter, serving me a cool glass of juice. He opened the groceries, took out six slices of bread, slapped a piece of meat on three slices, trimmed the meat to fit the bread and placed the other slice on top cutting each sandwich diagonally. He grinned, "See, that's all he needs, simple, tidy and easy." He put one sandwich on a plate and placed it in front of me. He took a bite out of his sandwich, and as Ty appeared around the corner from his office, put a sandwich in his hand and we all chowed down like old friends. They were warm and friendly, and two hours went by unnoticed, and yes, even Ty stayed the whole time) in an enjoyable conversation.

I commented, "You two look close to being twins, very tall, slim, dark wavy hair and warm brown eyes." They put their arms over each other's shoulders and Ty said "I'm the shortest and stockiest, just under six feet. The other nine brothers are over six feet. Aside from that, we all look very much alike. I think our Papa cloned us." Richard laughed, "I'm the oldest. I turned out so perfectly wonderful, that they fashioned all the brothers after me, except Ty. They patted him on top of the head often because he was so darned cute, making him a little shorter than the rest." "What about your father?" I asked. The reply "Same same only grey hair, and he wears it longer. He always wears a cowboy hat, inside and outside the house. That may be considered bad manners, but it suits him."

I left, agreeing to come back tomorrow to spend a little time with Richard, to make sure I felt comfortable in the kitchen.

Chapter Three

The Job

The days continued. I was now on first name basis with the store owners. His name was Mike and his wife's Betty. They had food already packaged for me, and bread picked out. The highest quality meat was cut just right for stews and casseroles. They packaged dried fruit and nuts to put out on the counter for the midnight marauder, and my smoothies were a big hit. Life was good.

Still, the air felt increasingly odd. Even Ty looked with concern at the sky. I told him how his brother described it and he agreed, "Never better explained." It made me uneasy.

In short bursts of time, Ty and I had quick conversations. He was much friendlier than I expected, and he had even shown me how to use his exercise machines. I was actually getting a little buff. Speaking of such, Ty had the muscles of a body builder and ran for three or four hours morning and night. The more information I gathered, the more I realized what an extraordinary human being he was.

Oh, I was not impressed all that easily; it was the rest I learned about him. His enterprise here in Calgary was to find small businesses that were failing or faltering and build them from the ground up into great successes. His only prerequisite was that the owner of the business be open minded, flexible, and be able to put his trust in Ty. Since it was word of mouth, men walked through the door with trust in their hand. The payout was immense.

On a percentage basis, Ty was paid according to the success, which he banked in the States (an important note for the future story). This involved his many university degrees and previous experience, combined with his mind-bending insight to think outside the box. I was told there was no one like him, or ever would be. That was hard to wrap my brain around, knowing of some great minds of our century. Little did I know, my knowledge of him to this point only scratched the surface.

I felt like a character from a novel – all I did was go to the store for groceries but instead found myself serving food to a great mind. Not only that, the family members were some of the warmest and most gracious people I could ever want to meet. I got to know them through numerous phone conversations.

Back to business, I simply made my favorite food accompanied with a pre-made salad from our favorite store and received thank-you messages left on the counter. I left extra food here and there and the night gremlin always gobbled it up.

Sometimes I received a request to take a couple of days off – company from out of town. They had meetings regarding one of his other businesses. The only hint I got was from the grocer telling me that some well-muscled men were in the store picking up steaks and other food – enough for ten hungry men, and no, they didn't look like family. He said they were polite, but not forthcoming with any information about themselves.

Twice, Richard had come to Calgary and brought his wife, Mary-Ann, his teenage daughter, Sandra, and their two-year old, Rebecca. I noticed that Sandra played guitar and never talked on the phone, and Rebecca sat at her feet in complete fascination. Rebecca had huge brown eyes and thick curly dark hair down to her waist. She didn't say much but her eyes were very expressive. We gradually developed a mutual friendship and she was fun to be with.

Chapter Four

Now We Meet The End

The day was a blur, but "the stir" in the air was very strong. I was at the house but needed a few extras from the store. It was there that I received the phone call. I recognized Ty's voice, firm and urgent "drop everything and come back as quickly as you can. Put your foot to the floor and stop for nothing."

My heart was pounding as I pulled into the driveway. He was waiting on the front step and ran down to the car as I appeared around the corner.   He flung open the driver's door. "Come quickly – we're in great danger." I felt the ground thumping, no, more like an earthquake, shaking, and I heard deafening noise. He pushed me through an open door and shouted "Sit down – you're going for a long ride. Hang onto my feet and tuck yourself in so you don't hit your head or arms." Down, down, occasionally slowing slightly, hearing a door slam behind us. It wasn't like the door to a house; it was a steel hatch closing. Down, down, slam, slam – I lost track of time, feeling sick to my stomach, dizzy and in shock. Eventually the last hatch slammed and I found myself in a dimly lit room with computer monitors in front of me. "Sit still and gather yourself – I have some work to do" echoed in my ears. No problem there. I was frozen with fear.

I gradually became aware of my surroundings and the pictures on the monitors. Some were satellite images showing land masses exploding. I lost my breath when I saw Calgary disappearing piece by piece. I saw familiar landmarks going, one at a time. The scene was repeating itself, playing over and over, sometimes slowing down for detail.

When I came to much later, I was handed a bottle of water and I sipped. "You're ok", I heard Ty's voice, "but Canada is under attack. It has been completely destroyed – all of it – from the east to the west coast. All of it is gone and all Canadian citizens – melted from the heat of the blasts. We are in a bomb shelter far below the land, on the ocean floor. We are safe here. I built this refuge myself and it is completely self supporting, able to manufacture its own oxygen and grow its own food. You relax. I will be busy for the next few days, checking systems and securing the structure." "Is anyone else here?" I inquired in a shaky voice. The answer was "No."

I didn't ask because I feared the answer. How could he possibly have built such a bomb shelter? Who was doing this to Canada? Were there other countries affected? Yes, I certainly was Alice in Wonderland, slipped down the rabbit hole, and nothing was comprehensible. Everything around me for the next three and a half years was odd and unbelievable.

I developed a ....tic.......... of sorts ....I saw ....heads without bodies floating by me

18

.... very clear detail .... accompanied by a sickening feeling. Everything I did and everything I looked at was overshadowed with these images. When I reached for a bottle of water, I reached through the shadow of a head. Closing my eyes didn't help. I didn't remember sleeping. I doubt I slept.

I gradually made my way around the large shelter, learning how to turn on lights, finding where the food was kept, where I slept, where the bathroom was, where the machine room was, and where the equipment was that manufactured the oxygen we were breathing. The most surprising room was the garden, lush with vegetables and lettuce.

I always kept a flashlight with me because I didn't always know how to turn on a light. Knowing Ty's habits, I prepared food every three hours, picked up a bottle of water, and started down a tunnel, seeking him out in the far reaches of one of the rooms, where I found him in complete concentration on a piece of equipment. It was crucial that everything run smoothly.

This went on for days and days until, out of self preservation, decided I needed to know the date, the day of the week, and the time.

I voiced my request to Ty. The next time he came to the main room which consisted of a small kitchenette, a sitting area, a small bedroom through a door to the side, plus an office in one corner which contained the computer monitors, he created a calendar in the corner of one of the screens with a clock ticking the time, a.m. and p.m., and the calendar ticking off as each day passed. He started the calendar at the time we first arrived. I was startled to see how much time had already gone by; three months and eight days to be precise.

He made another improvement. He said he was confident the generators could handle it. In the main living area, he programmed the lights bright from seven a.m. until midnight, then dim for the night.

I was quite brazen with Ty by this time, so I suggested, in order to break up the week, we have hot Sunday dinners, and finger food Saturday nights. Further to that, if we reached civilization again I would like to accomplish something I had always dreamed about which would require his help. I would like to dance. I was a complete klutz but if Ty could raise businesses from sure collapse, surely he could make a dancer of me. So after many months, a dancer I was.

This was the beginning of survival.

You might be as fascinated as I was about a design in our underground 'home'. We had a toilet that flushed and a shower with warm water. The water was recycled, cleaned, and used again. All waste was eliminated through a tube onto the ocean floor.

Ty gave me a curious look one day when he came in and saw me staring at the computer. "Come with me," as he walked to the sitting area "I've been preoccupied and have neglected to show you something. There is a television mounted on the wall. You had told me you loved watching Poirot, Sherlock Holmes and Nero Wolfe so I bought a complete collection of each." He showed me how to insert the DVD and turn on the monitor. I dropped to the floor not stirring for at least one day and one night.

This time, he delivered the food and water.

Chapter Five

Living Somewhere Between The End and The New Beginning

One day, when Ty had enough of me glued to my movies, he thought of a new occupation; shooting. He guided me to a new room I had never seen before. He loaded a gun with blanks, placed it in my hand, and pointed to a target. As I had watched the actors do on television shows, I supported the gun with both hands, braced myself, and fired. What a kick back it had! I fired a few more rounds and started enjoying myself. Ty gave me a few pointers, showed me how to reload, how to clean a gun properly, and disappeared.

Eventually, I was given moving targets on a screen, different scenarios, with increasing difficulties. He wrote the programs as we went along. He knew how to keep himself motivated, and me as well. I went shooting every day for hours. It was basically a glorified video game. I was enjoying it so much that I hoped to shoot real bullets at real targets some day. Occasionally, Ty joined me in the shooting games; he was an awesome shot. I felt proud because he said the same about me.

Whatever I was doing, I stopped every three hours, made sandwiches, picked up water, and delivered it to him. We were dependent on each other, and I was happy to do my part.

At the end of the day I would relax in front of my favorite Poirot movies. Between movies, I would sometimes amuse myself by discovering more freezers containing new and varied food choices. I was astounded at the food Ty packed in the shelter – a whole freezer full of bread, another with vegetables, another with dinner meat and sandwich meat from our favorite neighborhood store. No one mentioned he was buying extra slices of meat. Come to think of it, maybe he roasted it himself on the barbecue I saw on the patio. I did see a professional meat slicer on the counter .... ?

I had heard a comment that we use only a small portion of our brain. I had come to the conclusion that Ty had all of his brain cells up and functioning. I also discovered that he hardly ever slept. He said he had never required much sleep – just a few minutes here and there, and not too often. He rested and rejuvenated mostly through regular meditation. Most of his inventions and insights came to him this way.

One day I was making one of my usual food deliveries, when I found him in the air supply chamber in great distress. "You need to get the first aid kit from the white cabinet in the corner." I brought it over and opened it. He instructed me how to sterilize my hands, place masks on both of us, then sterilize his hands. That's when I nearly passed out. He told me firmly that our lives depended on me pulling myself together. The thumb on his right hand was pretty well severed. He didn't lose his

23

grip. There was a tendon that had to be sewn together or he would lose the use of his hand altogether. He explained, "A piece of equipment flew back at me. We have three day's supply of air. I need to do the repair quickly and I need my right hand to do it." "Is there anything I can do?" I inquired. "Just focus on my hand" was his reply.

He instructed me on threading a needle with the strongest thread. He held the tendon going up his arm to his shoulder and I very carefully took the other part. I secured the end with the thread – I needed a thimble to push the needle through the tough fibre. Sometimes I had to use small pliers supplied in the box. Since I enjoyed hand sewing in the past, I put my skills to use making short stitches up as far as I could go, then back down to the severed end. It took a while. He then had to manipulate his fingers on his end of the fibre until I could secure the end with thread and start sewing the second part. I knotted it on either side of the joint, hopefully making it more secure, then up towards his fingers. It was hard to get him to release his grip so I could sew further up the tendon but he finally released it. I went up as far as I could go. I asked if the thread might sever the fibre, but he assured me it was very strong and once I secured it, it wouldn't tear; the thread I was using was man-made but similar to a tendon in strength.

I finally came back down to the joint and secured it on the other side with a firm knot.

"How have you managed to not pass out?" I asked. "Training" he replied. That was worth a conversation a few days ahead.

We then used another kind of thread to sew the skin together. When finished, he started to flex his thumb and I snapped "Let it have a few days to heal – I'm not sewing it again if you break it." "It's not going anywhere with the way you've sewn it. I'm sure it has superior strength to any tendons in my body" he laughed. I had no idea how he could laugh at a time like this. I felt like passing out.

I staggered out the door and down the hall to the kitchen returning with a few juice boxes. I was ashamed to say that he was the one severely injured, but I was the one who passed out. When I awoke a few hours later, we were both in the living area. This was another one of those times when I didn't ask questions. How did he get me to the living area, and was the air chamber up and running? No, I would find out – the easy way or the hard way.

Chapter Six

Almost There

A few weeks later we sat cross-legged on the kitchen floor to eat our hot meal of the day as we always did.

Ty flexed his thumb explaining that he needed to keep it flexible. "I think it's even stronger than the other thumb" he remarked. "I owe you thanks every day for the rest of my life."

"Let's not get into that" I grinned. "I'm still alive and breathing. I'm an awesome shot, I dance well, and I watch my favorite movies every night. …. There's something I wonder about." It was very uncommon for me to ask any questions on the premise that I might not want to hear the answer but I took a chance. "I feel some sort of movement at all times. What does that mean – that I really feel movement, or that I'm crazy?"

"Not the latter" he replied. "This unit has small feet that are gradually walking us toward land – the States. Some of the shoreline is gone and it is mostly cliffs. I can see that on the satellite images. We will have to be hoisted from the water when we reach that point. I have been in constant contact with my team, always by encrypted messages. They're expecting us and are prepared to pull us to the surface. I expect it will be six months or less. We're moving very slowly. Not one of my best designs. I have kept track of our progress through satellite, and so has the team."

"I don't know how to take this all in" was all I could manage to say; then after a while, "Your team?".

I'm a Seal, actually SSF, Seal Special Force. There are only two teams. They consist of men with highly developed individual skills, as well as highly evolved senses beyond the five senses." You could bet I had nothing to say then. I had never been so astounded.

"That is why I owe you thanks each and every day. You have kept me going, bringing food, motivating me, and most importantly, restored my thumb. I'm first and foremost a Seal. The other businesses provide mind flexibility and entertainment, and often cover for our operations."

He continued, "The SSF are the visitors who came to the house for regular meetings. Which brings me to the thanks; I head my team. I am required to be the best, always the top of my game. We carry out missions that no one else can do; we do the impossible, and very successfully. Without my thumb, actually if I lost the tendon, it would mean the loss of my whole right arm, I would be nothing. Maybe that seems melodramatic to you, but I live my life to head the SSF. If I'm not that, I am done. That is why I consider you my angel."

He went on, "My team and I have been gathering information over the past three years. Actually, this mission started long before that, but our enemies pushed up operations. Therefore, we lost Canada. It's our first failure, and it will be the last. We have discovered that there are pods throughout the world, working together, and they're very dangerous. My team, along with the other SSF team, have disabled some of them, but there is much work to be done. We haven't reached many of the people responsible for Canada, and we won't quit until we're satisfied. They are dangerous, but we are more dangerous."

As predicted, a few months later, we were lifted by huge cranes onto a series of flatbeds, emerging to see the first sunlight we had experienced in three years, five months, and twenty-one days. Richard and I locked eyes. I tried not to cry but the tears started to flow.

SECTION TWO

THE NEW BEGINNING

Chapter One

The Secret

The next few days were lost.

Personal note: There are certain experiences in my life that I have learned to store in a compartment in my brain, lock it, and throw away the key. One of the subjects I haven't talked about in this book, is how I feel about losing all the wonderful people in this world who have had their lives cut short; it is locked away. When I die, whatever you do, don't crack my brain open. It could be Pandora's Box. (I mean the last two sentences as a joke).

I do remember that some of my family and closer friends were travelling at the time of the great disaster, but as yet I have not been able to locate them. However, there is a thread of hope.

I didn't really lose the first days of The New Beginning, I just didn't remember much, or at least it was muddled. I felt so overwhelmed, seeing sunlight, adjusting to the knowledge that I would not spend the rest of my life in a bomb shelter, meeting the members of what were to become my extended family, seeing the underwater bomb shelter on top of the flatbeds ....you get it.

Let's try starting here. Ty and I had played a game at meals to pass some time. He would ask me, if I could build my own house, any way I wanted it, down to the decorating and furniture, what would I build? We schemed for hours. He got in the fun of it by adding his ideas as well. The end result was a combined home. The top four levels were mine, the bottom three sub-basements were his. He could have put offices in the ranch house, but the small house would provide a discreet cover for his operations.

I was sure he, too, needed time to adjust to the 'real world' again, so he and his team built the home of my dreams before they went forth with their more important work.

It's not anything you would imagine, I'm sure. After all, if one is imagining something, why not dream big? No, not me; I like it cozy. I wanted a rather small house, at least small floor space on each level, but a few levels. By the time they added Ty's requests as well, the house had seven levels, three above ground, one basement (a walk-out to the garden), and three sub-basements.

The lowest three floors, sub-basements, are Ty's office, with accommodations for his team members on the two floors above that. (In his previous life, I think Ty must have been some creature who lived in tunnels underground).

30

All joking aside, it provides the safest and most inconspicuous place for his operations.

Then, moving to the roof top, you will find my private room – a secret room that only I can access; a retreat. A panel in my bedroom wall slides aside, allowing access to the elevator, which is activated by my iris and my thumb print. The elevator is a very tight fit, just for one. It goes one storey up (to the roof top) and is very cleverly disguised from the outside of the house, looking like part of the design of the solar panels. You would never know the roof concealed an upper room. Everything was lowered into the room then the roof and solar panels were installed over top. They worked on that part at night.

This room is wonderful; the smell of the hardwood floor (which has a brightly covered Indian rug in the middle), the luxury of the ornate roll top desk, the bay window surrounded by plush window seating which provides a very relaxing place to sit and look out over the garden and fish pond. There is also a full bath, a small fridge, and a dumb waiter (I have a fondness for snacks). They also provided the room with an overstuffed sofa opposite the desk (great for naps). Only Ty and his team know about it, and there is no one more trustworthy to keep a secret.

Speaking of secrets, I have a request of you, the reader. I ask that you honor the fact that the SSF does not exist on any records and the troops are not recorded either. They don't exist.

I too remain nameless, as I was in the bomb shelter designed and operated by the Captain of the SSF team. My existence would be tracked back to Ty which would lead back to the SSF team. If that information leaked out, there would be severe consequences. At the time of the great disaster, Canadians were abroad on vacation and business. (Thank goodness some still exist in this world). However, I am the one and only Canadian who was actually in Canada at that time, and who is still alive today.

There is another reason for your discretion. Ty trained me to be among the best of the shooters in the States, next to the two shooters, twins, who are right now on loan to the other SSF team and who are carrying out missions abroad. For now, I have joined the team as an honorary shooter, to carry out missions on U.S. soil. You will never hear my name.

Chapter Two

My First Home

I digress. I was talking about the house that was built for me. I want to go into great detail on my home, as it's the first one I've ever owned and I'm very proud of it. I've already described my private room so I'll start again on the lowest sub-basement (the seventh floor) in more detail and work my way up.

The seventh floor has a spacious, bright office with several large computer monitors in a semi-circle, with one chair for the controller. There are many satellite images in real time, with surveillance on all continents. Magnified spots show all pods considered dangerous. There is also surveillance on the ranch and the vast land surrounding it and also surveillance on Washington. The office is protected by thick walls and the door has a secure locking system (very much like a bank vault). Outside the office is a comfortable, dimly lit seating area. Twelve lounge chairs circle a large coffee table, with a monitor built into the table top, designed for conducting meetings. Adjoining this room is a large bathroom with all the luxuries, including a whirlpool bath. Actually, all bathrooms in the house are equipped pretty much the same. This floor also contains a room housing a generator, air filtering system and a water cleaning system.

The sixth and fifth floors have six bedrooms each with luxurious baths, and a lounge area to one side. We schemed, while deep in the shelter on the ocean floor, that basements can be gloomy (I wonder what made us think of that?) so we designed high ceilings, a clever lighting system (sometimes pillars, softly illuminated), plus a moving wall.

The moving wall is very much like an enormous television monitor, expanding from ceiling to floor, wall to wall. This feature wall has buttons to change the scenes: waterfalls, forests, oceans, aquariums, and gardens, complete with sound effects. The brightness can be adjusted as well. We became so enthused that we decided one wall in each room of the house would benefit by the same feature. When turned off, a curtain can be drawn, concealing the screen.

The fourth floor has an equipment room on the far end. This room contains a large back-up generator, a wall safe, and vacuflow. There is also a super-sized washer and dryer for bedding. The main room is a shooting gallery, much like the one in the underwater shelter, except the wall is designed to accommodate real bullets. I still practice daily.

The third and second floors are built like an open loft with a moving wall spanning the height of two floors. The third level is the ground floor (with a walk-out to the garden). Hidden behind a bamboo screen is a small kitchenette for simple needs such as a water cooler, coffee maker, fridge and other small appliances. The rest of the room is decorated in a garden atmosphere, with a stone floor and wicker furniture, complemented by plants such as large sweeping ferns and small palms.

French doors open onto a restful patio replicating a gazebo. Stone steps lead to a fish pond with underwater lighting, complete with an ever changing fountain. Surrounding it is a breathtaking garden that lights up at night giving a mystical atmosphere. It extends all the way to the canyon. My favorite part of the special effects lighting is cleverly designed fairies fluttering in the trees. I can see them from my private room.

My love for palm trees lead to imported palms of different types and sizes, often utilizing grow lights and native soil to help them thrive. Trent, the family horticulturist, was very active in planning and maintaining the garden. He also imported tropical plants with bright and unusual flowers. Sections are dedicated to categories such as arid, evergreen, fruit bearing plants and trees, hanging gardens, and a restful Japanese garden. Trent also installed a small green house for tomatoes, green peppers, and herbed plants such as basil and rosemary.

Entering the house again on the third floor, you will find carpeted stairs leading up to the second floor which is a library. Book shelves line one wall, with a ladder that moves on a track, enabling readers to reach the top shelves easily. The room has soft beige carpeting, and slightly darker sofas and chairs with lamps over each chair. The moving wall from the balcony view is breathtaking – if you can only imagine the expanse of the waterfall, or a full wall of aquarium with exotic fish. It has a 3-D effect adding depth to the picture; absolutely awesome!

The first floor has a full kitchen, and an island with bar stools along one side. I like a casual atmosphere; no table; just sit on the stools. (It's almost as good as sitting cross-legged on the floor as we did in the shelter). There are two patio doors shaped in arches. One is in the kitchen, the other in the living room. One of the patio doors opens onto a large balcony where I can sit with a cup of coffee while enjoying a view of the ranch house in the distance.

My bedroom is next to the patio door. There is a privacy screen just inside the door to hide the room from the kitchen. A magnificent mahogany sleigh bed is in the centre of the room, with multi-colored bohemian designed satin bedding. The ceiling is lit with twinkling stars and soft lighting. The elevator to the secret room is accessed from a panel on one wall. There is, of course, a moving wall that I enjoy every night, programmed to nature sounds and dim lighting. Adjoining is a large luxurious bathroom. The floor and fixtures are mostly white marble adorned with gold taps.

On the opposite wall of the kitchen, wide carpeted stairs lead to a sunken living room. This room has plush built-in seating on three walls, with an over-stuffed crescent-shaped sofa on the remaining wall. The moving scenery is not necessary in this room, so a large television is mounted on the far side, where I enjoy my murder mysteries. A patio door looks out over the garden. The arched doorways are built of blue glass tiles. Matt tiles, blue, beige and soft yellow in color continue throughout the kitchen and most of the living room; dramatic and cheery.

When the house was completely finished, Ty gave me the tour, explaining how to work the moving walls, the television, the lights, the laundry facilities and so on. At the end of the tour, he took me back to the kitchen, pointing out a locked drawer. He opened it, showing me three separate bank books. One was for Boston, one for the closest town, and one for a town in the next county. The balances were enormous. He told me he had good earnings from his business in Canada, sending some home for 'ranch business', while banking the rest in Boston. He split the difference and shared with me, as he felt I needed a good start here. "A good start!" I exclaimed, "That's a fortune! Why would you give it to me?" He simply answered "It's more than I'll ever need." With that he left me to examine my new home, which, as I said, is the first four floors of a much larger building.

Are you bored? I could talk about my home for pages, but I'll be nice and go on with the rest of the story. It's quite exciting in parts. There's my job as a shooter - an extraordinary and unusual experience.

Chapter Three

The Job

Just as I was getting settled and learning to enjoy my luxury, I observed Ty walking toward me from the ranch house. He was walking with a purpose, absorbed in thought, and I knew instinctively that 'business' was about to begin.

Upon entering the kitchen, he said "We have a mission tonight. We will carry out all operations under a night sky. These two guns are very similar to the one you have been using for practice, but with a few upgrades. They have eight chambers instead of the usual six, they're coated with a matt paint making them invisible at night, and they're virtually silent firing. A very unique design feature is that a flash will not be visible when fired. I also have this suit for you to wear on each mission, and night vision glasses as well. Here is a bullet belt to carry reloads. All of this equipment will render you invisible at night. It absorbs all light and all that can be seen is a black hole. Be careful to avoid street lights, and all other lights because the enemy will see a silhouette of blackness. Suit up and load, target practice for sixteen rounds, reload, then meet the team for a briefing in my office."

In the briefing, each of the troops was assigned a job according to his own unique skills. Ty told me to wait at a small discreet x on the ground. When it disappeared I was to follow dim laser light flashes until I came to another x, stand still and look straight ahead. For each short blast of the laser I was to shoot once on that exact spot. The rule was one shot per target; don't miss. "No problem," I thought, "it's just exactly like the games in the shooting gallery down to every detail." When I pulled the suit on, I found it was light weight and flexible. Completely suited up, I looked in the mirror and started. My goodness, I couldn't see a thing. I was a virtual black hole. That was eerie!

We loaded into the waiting helicopter. I found it amazing that it made no noise at all. Invention has come a long way. No one spoke. When we landed, each team member silently slipped to the ground and went his predetermined way. My senses were heightened. I felt like I could even hear myself blink. I found my x and as it disappeared I followed my trail, stopping on the second x. I looked intently ahead. Flashes of light; pop, pop. I knew I hit the mark each time because the light promptly disappeared. No more flashes, I stood still until Ty strode up beside me. We went home, debriefed, were told our mission went like clockwork, and separated. I immediately went to the shooting gallery, cleaned my guns, locking them in the cabinet. Ty found me and took my suit for cleaning, making it ready for the next mission.

I was still hyped so I strolled in the garden. I mused about the suit and the effect it had. The guns didn't even flash when fired; I couldn't get over that. The glasses hid my eyes. It was awesome. Maybe I could write a comic book. There's Superman, there's Spiderman, there's the Green Lantern, there's the Black Hole. Do you think it would fly? If Ty knew I was carrying on so, I'm sure he would relinquish my privileges.

There were many missions similar to that one. Ty always came to me carrying my equipment. "Suit up." was all he said, and the routine began. On one mission, I heard a bullet hit the ground in front of me, throwing dirt in my face. It was a rather bright night. Someone must have seen my outline. I crouched down and took out the rest of my targets from that position. No one said a word going back home, but I knew the Black Hole almost bit the dust that night.

.

Chapter Four

The Family

I was getting to know the family by now. Papa and his ten sons are remarkable. I expected country people, dressed in casual, well worn clothing as they went about their work, but I guess from the influence of the nearby towns which I discovered are wealthy and upscale, combined with their university education, the men (including Papa) wear nice fitting black jeans and fitted shirts, always pressed. That's how Ty dressed in Canada, and Richard looked when he came for a visit, but I thought it was 'dress-up' for the city. Ty often wore navy blue, beautifully tailored suits in the office (he looked drop-dead gorgeous behind his mahogany desk).

Papa's too busy to be friendly. French doors with beveled glass panels open into his office, where you can always find him seated behind a large walnut desk with matching chair his father had built for him, as well as the two matching 'customers' chairs facing the desk. Another set of French doors open out onto a flower garden. (Trent, the horticulturist, recently included some palms; they became very popular with the family, and with future designs he and Thomas, the architect, partnered on). Papa is very fussy about his looks. He is tall and slim, dresses in black jeans, fitted shirts, cowboy boots and hat. Richard told me he's very fussy about his hair. He has it cut to suit his hat then puts his hat on to have it checked for length and style. Now that's fussy!

Papa made sure all of his sons received university educations, just as his father did for him. Most of them have more than one degree.

Richard is the oldest son. He met his wife, Mary-Ann in university, both studying foreign trade; her focus being textiles and his being cattle and equipment ... and Mary-Ann. Soon he was wearing fitted shirts, unique in color and design (made by Mary-Ann). They were married upon graduation. Mary-Ann, whom I had first met in Canada, became a dressmaker/tailor, opening a shop in town. She designs clothes for the neighboring four towns, and shirts for the 'boys' in the family.

They each have their own style and color preference, all fitted perfectly for each individual. In addition, she makes tailored suits for each of them. (She designed Ty's suits that I had seen in Canada).

I found out in later experiences, that the boys sometimes exchanged shirts, just for fun, making them hard to identify. Sometimes Papa would give work instructions for a certain job to the wrong son, ending in loud laughter when the mistake was discovered.

I have told you about Ty. He is the second oldest.

Thomas is the architect and builder. You will hear about his work later in this story. He works closely with Trent on all projects.

Will is a long haul trucker and family lawyer. He is the other brother who chose matrimony. No wonder! His wife, Catherine, is a beautiful, tiny blond, with a very pleasing personality. They met in university, both graduating from law, but chose alternate professions after graduation. They have two children: Eric, fourteen and Sophie, ten. She has the bakery in town next to Mary-Ann's dressmaking shop. Her parents are of Polish decent and own a bakery in Manhattan. That is where Catherine learned the trade. Her children are already pretty good bakers themselves, mostly producing kid-friendly cookies. She bakes amazing pastries, European style, often including a silky chocolate on (or in) each of the creations. No one in the family bothers to bake; Catherine supplies them with whatever their heart desires. Her children are just like her; blond, sweet, and friendly. They came immediately to me, crowding around and telling me their stories of the fun they have in the bakery. Daddy joins them too whenever he's in town. They giggle about his misadventures with cookies.

Paul is the hairstylist and shoemaker. The next four brothers are accountant (Alan), veterinarian (Michael), electrician and real estate agent (Roger), horticulturist (Trent), and the youngest, Steven, is the chef.

The house itself is beautiful. I imagine it was Papa's wife's doing. It has a very large professional kitchen, with a counter lined with bar stools on one side, especially handy for shift workers coming in at all times of the day or night. They have formal dinners in the dining room only on Sundays. Past the kitchen is the spacious dining room with a large table, seating thirty, if needed. When I first saw it, I thought it was to accommodate the spouses and children, but only two are married, each with two children. Papa said they are just too focused on their work to be able to accommodate marriage.

I had to ask! Yes, son Steven and partner Sean have formal education as chefs, frequently travelling to Italy and France.

The 'boys' are all slim, some slightly bulkier like Ty, but his bulk is all muscle. At least, I thought that to be the case until I was at the ranch house one day for dinner, when they offered to show me their work-out room, as I complained that I was getting a little 'soft' and needed to muscle up a bit. Oh man! This whole bunch is muscled! They are all enthused about their work-out machines and weight lifting equipment. No wonder Ty had a gym in the house in Canada; it came with the territory. The whole sub-basement in the ranch house is a gym, each individual having contributed some of the machines as new and better ones came onto the market. Even

Papa, I discovered, takes time out of his busy schedule for daily workouts, apparently twice a day (and he runs too; they have races). Sandra is right in there with the men as well! I found that out when I went for a work-out one day.

I know Ty doesn't sleep much, and noticed the kitchen staff are there 24/7, but it was confirmed in conversation at the dinner table that none of them require much sleep. They said their grandfather was the same. He taught them if they lived their life right, got proper nutrition and regular exercise, they would run like a well oiled machine. I would like to have met him.

Now it was all starting to come together. Each son had a certain amount of work on the ranch, but each also had his own business, or businesses, coordinated by Papa from his office. Twice a day, Richard took over while his father went for a workout, then tended to sick cattle in the barn. He showered, returned looking like a fashion model, and took over his coordinating job, refreshed.

I haven't talked much about Mary-Ann on a personal level. She is slightly aloof and speaks her mind which doesn't always make her terribly popular. She has long dark curly hair and green/blue eyes. Her figure is what I would call voluptuous and she always looks stunning in the dresses she designs for herself. She is a very hard working lady and according to Sandra, a great wife and mother, making sure they sit down to dinner together every evening. She always took Sandra to work with her when she was young, and now its Rebecca's turn. Both girls know a lot about dressmaking and help with the children's clothing line.

Chapter Five

Blue Martini

I eventually became familiar with the surroundings. I found a farmer's market within walking distance. I like a fellow named Harry. His booth is not as fancy as the others but he can sure grow vegetables and fruit. He is particularly talented at making fruit/veggie drinks and I buy a glass each time I go there.

I don't know how we got into the conversation but it came down to "I don't drink alcohol but if I could have a drink, it would be a blue martini." His reply was that he would work on it for me. One day he presented me with a fancy bottle and an exquisite martini glass. He said it took twenty-nine fruits, vegetables and edible flowers to come up with the right color and flavor, then a series of filtering to get the color a clear, beautiful blue. I took it home and tried it and found he was right on the money.

I had heard he was rather poor so I went back the following weekend with some fancy wine bottles for future bottling, and offered to pay the going rate for good wine if he would fill the bottles with the blue juice. He said it was quite a process and it would take some time but he would call when it was ready. True to his word, he delivered right to my door. I knew it was an expensive and labor intensive process so I paid him fifty dollars a bottle. He didn't want to take that much, but I convinced him that it was the usual price the family paid for good wine at the dinner table. So the Blue Martini immerged.

The uncanny thing was that I was feeling healthier, more alert and all over absolutely amazing after a few bottles. The 'floating heads' were even less frequent. Ty tried it, then the chefs in the kitchen, all with the same conclusion. Whatever farmer Harry was bottling was an amazing product.

With a little coaxing on my part at a family dinner one Sunday night, the two chefs introduced themselves to Harry and offered their help in producing and bottling the Blue Martini because one man alone couldn't keep up with the demand. They quickly purchased equipment – bottle washers, filtering system, juicers and other pieces to increase production. They paid for the improvements out of their own pockets and kept his formula private, giving all proceeds to Harry.

My talented friend was able to afford to move into a nice home (their former home was in complete disrepair and even had holes in the roof and walls). His two children began doing much better in school. The family started giving them nice clothing to wear, which increased their confidence. It wasn't just that, it showed Harry's family that people cared and wanted them to get ahead.

It was a sweet deal. Farmer Harry thrived, we received regular deliveries of Blue Martini and we all became healthier. Blue Martini was now served at the dinner table instead of the regular wine.

Another amazing thing happened because of the Blue Martini. Papa started drinking it in his office, instead of the scotch. He even used a fancy martini glass. He had one client who came every Thursday. They drank scotch together and had for years. Papa offered him the martini and the fellow almost walked out on him. He finally convinced him "just one sip then I'll pour you a double scotch." The fellow's expression changed as he finished the glass (which by now was always served in the standard martini glass). He asked for a refill. Now its Blue Martini Thursdays at Papa's. What's even more amazing is that the client's health had been failing and he didn't expect to live much longer. He now has a twinkle in his eye, a good word to say, and a clean bill of health. Both Papa's and the client's dispositions have greatly improved as a by-product of Blue Martini. Imagine that.

Chapter Six

Who Am I? ... and ... I'm in Business

By now, I'm sure you're wondering how I'm introducing myself to the community. Well, the chef in the kitchen, Steven, is gay and the fellow working with him is his partner. The two are very gifted with food, always smiling and joking, turning out the best quality and imaginative cuisine served anywhere. The family pays them well and they are most appreciated. Although they run the kitchen twenty-four-seven, they get along famously, and Sean, his significant other, is on the short side with blond hair.

Perfect. I'm his sister. I spent a lot of hours belly up to the kitchen counter (an island, similar to my kitchen only much larger, with ten bar stools facing the kitchen itself, accommodating shift workers coming and going to their respective jobs). Sean is delightful, and we talked extensively about his childhood and university days ... you get it.

These lovely men deliver food to my kitchen every evening (unless there is a family dinner at the ranch house), and knowing I'm a snacker, a plate of delectable snacks for the evening as a bonus, while, yes, I'm still watching my Poirot, Sherlock, and Nero movies. Sometimes I just stare at the moving wall, or lounge in the garden with a selection from the snack plate. Life is good.

51

One day at the farmer's market, a particularly inquisitive, elderly neighborhood lady remarked that everyone in the family was very ambitious and she understood they all had their own business. We sorted it all out. Papa coordinated everyone as well as running 'ranch affairs'. Three worked for the family, one as a chef in the ranch kitchen, and two as accountants, billing and ordering, keeping ledgers. The rest were an electrician and real estate agent, an architect and builder, a long haul trucker (and company lawyer), and one is even a hair stylist, working out of a salon at the ranch house, and on we went. That took care of all ten men. There was a little white lie about Ty (there is only one accountant).

This gave me some time to think ahead for the answer I knew I would need. Sure enough "and what, my dear, do you do?" It was a little bit of a stretch, but true enough without putting a name on it until now. "I have a wonderful tea garden at the rear of my house, backing onto the canyon. It is beautifully lit at night and most enjoyable and restful day or evening. When anyone needs a breather, they sit by the fish pond with the ever-changing fountain and I serve coffee and snacks. It's a service they were very much in need of."

Oh boy, I didn't think this one through! Whenever you tell a lie, even a little white one, you need to be prepared to back it up. You've guessed it. Myrtle went on, "I would love to see your garden, and I have some friends too.   Seven of us seniors have a quilting club."   Oh great, you can't fool seniors.   They're always one step ahead and can smell a 'story' from a mile away.

"Well," I replied "the family keeps me busy with their needs, but I suppose we could set up a visit for you and your friends. I'd love to meet them.   The evening would be preferable; a tour with the lights is most impressive."

Myrtle called two days later to make arrangements.   I alerted Steven and Sean. They dressed in black shirts with white pants, draped a crisp white linen towel over one arm, and served champagne, Blue Martini and delectable finger foods. The evening was a great success and Sean and I were able to keep our 'story' straight.

We all knew what that was leading to.

We set Friday evenings aside and opened the garden to the neighborhood. Revisions had to be made to the garden to accommodate our visitors, but there were never more than twenty in one evening, and they came and went (open-house style).

I was now in business.

It turned out to be a 'good mistake'. I was able to meet the neighbors in an intimate setting, getting to know each and every one in a very enjoyable fashion.

It picked up Mary-Ann's dressmaking business as well. She would often do a fashion show for adults and children, and receive orders that kept her hopping. I love her designs and wear nothing but 'Mary-Ann'.

Whenever my, um, other work, takes me away, the family pitches in. Mary-Ann and her two girls are particularly helpful. I have become closest with Richard's family, and with my two partners-in-crime in the kitchen.

So, out of a white lie sprung a very enjoyable business that brought happiness to the whole family, and the entire neighborhood.

Chapter Seven

The Formidable Seven

At our garden parties, we served champagne as well as our famous blue drink. We discovered that the quilting ladies liked to get a little tipsy. That made me nervous, and often a member of the family had to load them up and deliver them to their door. I wasn't at all happy about it, so with farmer Harry's help, he stepped up production of Blue Martini, allowing the blue drink to be served exclusively.

One Friday evening is one I'll never forget. All had gone home, the cleaning was finished, and I sat in the kitchen with a cup of green tea. I heard someone crying outside my front door and went out to find one of the group of seven, Alice, sitting on the porch swing in an inebriated and most upset state. I sat with her and talked for a long time. She had never admitted to anyone previously, but after her husband died, she felt so lonely in her large, beautiful home that she turned to alcohol. She had obviously gone home from the party and got smashed. I excused myself and returned with a bottle and two martini glasses and we drank the night away; Blue Martini. We giggled when I told her about my white lie that turned into a lucrative business, simply because I didn't want to be perceived as unambitious. Upon daybreak, I called over to Sean and he delivered her home with a supply of Blue Martini. She was rather frail that evening, but with the help of the healthy drink, became a going concern.

During our conversation, I mentioned that it would give her, and her six friends, purpose in their lives to go to the school and teach the 'young ones' how to quilt, and perhaps other skills they might have to pass on. I knew the principal of the school to be open-minded and flexible, and thought she would accommodate any classes they suggested.

Well, that opened the box! Quickly, they were teaching quilting, needlework, gardening, and more. One wiry lady, Yvonne, was a very capable landscaper. That's what she did 'back in the day' with her husband. The school set up a program where they picked one block in a nearby town, and landscaped each and every front yard on the entire street. Next semester, it was the next block. Often the owners joined in the adventure and everyone became very proficient at landscaping. It also cultivated great friendships, old and young. Can you imagine? -- A whole town of landscapers. This endeavor lead to other community activities.

Whenever you saw the group of seven ladies marching up to the school, or a business, or down someone's street, you knew they wouldn't take 'no' for an answer. They simply didn't accept it. They became influential and very powerful.

I named them 'The Formidable Seven' at one of our parties in the back garden, and they loved it. They developed an organization of sorts, calling themselves by that name. The Mayors of the surrounding towns organized a fair in their name, honoring them for their work. It made the group even more powerful, and a lot of good came to the surrounding communities as a result.

The ladies still found time to meet with me regularly, sometimes on a week night if Friday was taken. Mary-Ann has become a welcome part of the group as well. I felt I was one of their lost lambs and a part of their strong bond. Alice and I eventually told the group how the 'garden parties' began and we all had a great laugh.

Chapter Eight

Something is Astir

I didn't see Richard very often, but we were special friends. All of the boys worked practically around the clock and thrived on it. Anyone with a family valued it and put time aside to keep a close relationship with their spouse and children. They were a remarkable group of people.

One afternoon, Richard walked into my kitchen when I was enjoying a quiet moment with a cup of green tea. He poured a cup for himself and pulled up to the kitchen island.

He looked me firmly in the eyes and said quietly "something is astir." I went cold. He continued "No, not like before, a different stir. Before you, it was every man for himself. We saw that farmer Harry and his family were suffering but it didn't occur to us to help. There were other families in the neighboring towns with problems and we didn't 'interfere'."

"Leading by example, your first project was making friends with farmer Harry, then you pointed out to us at the dinner table one evening that he couldn't keep up with the demand for Blue Martini and asked for our help. Of course, anything for you. Briefly into our new project, we started noticing a light in our eyes we had never seen before and vocalized that. Farmer Harry and his family had the light too and quickly thrived. Then you worked your magic on the quilting ladies, and next thing you knew the neighborhood was buzzing, and our children had new energy and enthusiasm. It spread quickly through the four neighboring towns."

Little did they know, it was the Canadian spirit, but I couldn't talk of it.

Richard continued, "The air is different now. Everyone I speak to talks about it, and talks about you. I told you the first day I met you that I thought you were an Angel. Upon arriving here, the family quickly saw something very special in you and started calling you 'Angel' as well. We would like your permission to formally change your name."

He went on, "The Mayors in the four neighboring towns would like to plan another fair, this time in your name and all four men want to make speeches to honor you. They have been working long and hard on a special gift for your garden."

I blinked tears away. I couldn't believe my ears. From where I came, I did nothing, lived for myself, and it was a big stretch to even make meals for Ty. When did I change? I voiced this to Richard and he just smiled and replied "You were an Angel who was dormant, just waiting to spread your wings and make a mark in this life." He put his arm around me and soon his shoulder was soggy. When I composed myself again, I shook my head and offered a towel, saying that it was dangerous to get that close to me. Angels are enthusiastic criers. "Richard, I don't see myself as an Angel, or to be called such or honored as such. I'm just plodding along, trying to survive the aftermath of a vast tragedy." He replied "Get used to it, Angel." Then he finished his tea and left.

"Something is astir alright" I remarked out loud to the air. "I can shoot with the SSF, I can make myself at home in a new country, I can mould myself into a member of a remarkable family, who by the way, are all a good foot taller than me, making me feel like Alice in Wonderland, however, I can't handle it when they want to make me an honorary Angel. That's something you become when you die and hopefully end up in heaven. I wonder how that will work for me, since I shoot people for a living, and to top it off, with a feeling of revenge. I don't complain about the past, but it sure takes over my emotions when it comes to shooting bad guys. That's what fuels me, gives me a very strong motive to carry on. It's secretly what I live for, and what makes me a deadly accurate shot." My speech to myself was finished and I was very tired.

I slept on it and woke up the next day being addressed as 'Angel', smiling back in appreciation. After all, an Angel would handle the situation with grace. I knew this would never **ever** change me. I am too much about my past, struggling along, trying to deal with whatever life hands me. I still have spells of 'floating heads' periodically. I am aware that I'm three parts crazy with my experiences of the recent past; I try to hide it, but at times it sneaks out. I don't hear anyone complaining about it, so I guess I won't either.

Chapter Nine

Glow in the Dark

I was growing a little weary of my job lately. I was always reliable, and a deadly shot, one per target. However, I seemed to have worked off some of the revenge that gave me the edge. Therefore, I was glad when the house phone rang, requesting my presence at the office. Down, down I went, to the seventh floor. The entire team was standing in the lounge area, with two additional men I had never met.

Ty told me that the other SSF team had their shooters trained now, enabling them to return Karl and Kent to our team. I was introduced, shook their hands, and made a mental note that they were not as they first appeared to be. First glance told me they were both about six-two, very skinny which made them look even taller, with white transparent skin, hair with no color, and light blue eyes. Shaking their hands, the impression changed to wiry, quick and strong, but the color up close looked even lighter. I stood for what seemed to be about five minutes looking at them, and them looking back. Everyone stood patiently and watched us. Finally, I turned to Ty with a twinkle and my best silly look, saying "You're going to have to dip them in something; they'll glow in the dark."

The first to laugh the longest and hardest were my two new friends. They said they'd never been described like that before. They assured me they had the same black suits I have, and glasses and guns identical. "I want to have a word with you about that later" I said. (Boy, what's the matter with me, rude and bossy!)

I turned to Ty again "I hope this means I have some time off, or maybe even retirement. I'm edgy lately; just not myself." He said he might need me occasionally, so keep in practice, but for the most part, my work was done and I could enjoy life.

Later, showing the two glow-sticks my beautiful garden (Honestly, I don't know what my problem is; I even **think** rude.) I dared to talk about my impression of the Black Hole, and how I thought it would make an excellent crime-fighter comic book. I added quickly that it was meant as a joke. "Think of what we feel like looking at each other, from very white, to a Black Hole at night. We have to touch elbows to keep in sync with each other on the job" Kent confided. "I like that Black Hole concept" said Karl grinning. "It puts humor into the job, and we need that with each other. The job can be so intense."

I assured them that I found the team to be totally professional, and so highly skilled that they don't have 'attitude'; nothing to prove. I recounted the time I had almost taken a bullet, and how not one of them commented. "I felt like we were in it together, supporting each other, backing each other up, confident in our respective skills. No one pointed a finger. You're with a good team, the best of the best in all respects, and from what I've heard about you from Ty, you're top shooters. I'm very happy to pass the torch back to you."

On a more humorous note, I asked them if I could call them Glow-sticks. They thought it was a cute and friendly way to greet each other; Angel and the Glow-sticks, turning into Black Hole Crime Fighters by night. They said they had never encountered someone who could hit the nail on the head without making them feel uncomfortable. "Hey fellas" I laughed "I'm a five-two blond woman with no training except for shooting. These strong burly men accepted me into their herd. You're tall, strong, trained and capable. If you take an honest look, they all come from different backgrounds. If that doesn't convince you, they walk around with martini glasses in their hands when they're here." The stage had been set with humor and that's exactly what one needs to shoot. You have to hang loose and have your brain on nothing but your target.

Any time we met thereafter, we shared a knowing grin, and often we would add to our verbal comic book of the Black Hole Crime Fighters. I still think it would be a great success.

Chapter Ten

One Last Hurrah

Ty stayed behind on intelligence and both SSF teams went overseas on missions. They were close to snaring everyone involved in 'the big disaster'. Ty spent day and night without sleep in front of the computer monitors in his office, coordinating operations. Richard occasionally joined him. Steven delivered food regularly, and I took Blue Martini in tall glasses periodically. Nothing keeps a man on his feet better than the blue juice.

It was very fortunate that he kept surveillance on the ranch house and the expanse of land owned by the ranch because he saw them coming; a small army of mercenary intent on wiping out the operation Ty was running, plus all family members.

He sent an SOS to his team, secured his office, then whipped upstairs with my equipment. "Suit up. We're in danger." He went on to find Richard. I didn't know until now, but Richard was SSF in his youth, but retired to have a wife and family. Ty had no intention of ever involving him again, but this was life or death.

I replied to the air "The last time I heard the word 'danger' from Ty, I slipped down a rabbit hole and spent three-and-a-half years as Alice in Wonderland. This can't be good." By the time I suited up, though, I gathered myself together, knowing there was room for no thought except for the target. I was very sure that whatever it was it could be my last day, but when called upon, that was the understanding.

I hurried into the front yard to find Richard and Ty. That was all, just three defenders. Ty briefed us very quickly. This would be different. The two men would take the flanks, and the shooter would go right down the centre, shooting anything that moved.

I was out of my element, but trusted the training would see me through. It was a very dark night, so I picked one bright star as my guide and proceeded forward. Soon enough I saw movement, squatted to use the night sky to determine silhouettes. Pop, pop, pop. No more movement so I pushed forward past the heaps on the ground, squatted, more silhouettes, pop, pop, pop.

I came to realize that they couldn't see either, so they carefully spaced themselves out and marched in threes. I kept count of bullets; after every twelve rounds, I reloaded, squatting next to a heap for cover.

Back out in the centre I saw the outline of three more and they were close. It was to my advantage that I was invisible. I braced myself and shot three more times. It unnerved me to have targets so very close, but I squared my shoulders and carried on. I loaded three more times in the same manner, each time dropping that portion of the empty ammunition belt.

They didn't realize what was coming because I got to each line before they could see their comrades on the ground. I had invisibility and the element of surprise on my side.

It seemed relentless, and I was tiring, and beginning to feel confusion. At this point, I couldn't see or hear anyone coming, but I didn't know if I could trust my senses. I crept forward cautiously. I jumped when I felt something touch me. It was a dog from the barns. They called him Benjamin. I heard they used him for tracking, and I soon learned why.

He led me forward, and when there was movement in front, he alerted me, using his pointing skills. That brave little soldier gave me a feeling of confidence and security.

Finally, he stretched up as tall as he could reach, his ears moving in all directions, like radar. When he confirmed there was no more movement, he nestled up beside me on the ground. I kept one arm ready to fire if needed.

After quite some time, I heard Ty's low whistle, then another whistle answer him. Benjamin ran to get the two boys to guide them to me. Ty pulled me up and guided me to a path along the canyon delivering me to my front step. Dawn was breaking.

I looked up and saw two choppers coming in. The teams took care of the clean-up. The satellite images recorded the entire night which helped with the records. The dropped ammo belts were useful in determining my movements. It came to their realization that, while we were attacking them overseas, they were attacking us on U.S. soil.

I had a long, hot shower, afterwards sitting by the fish pond for a few hours, Benjamin and Blue Martini as my companions. I was exhausted and in shock. Benjamin wanted to 'fish' in the pond, so I called the ranch kitchen for Steven to deliver a big bone. He managed to convince the enthusiastic dog that the fish were Angel's friends, and it was very bad manners to eat them.

Benjamin hung around a lot after that, protecting me. The boys even had to shampoo and fluff him, giving him a pretty blue collar. If anyone said "oh, you're a fru-fru dog" he would jump around with pleasure. If they didn't groom him each day, he would throw a brush in their direction; if that didn't get results, they would receive a sharp bark.

I recovered sufficiently, and Ty debriefed the teams. The 'flanks' silenced a few strays, but most of the mercenaries were right down the centre. They didn't realize the expanse of the operation until they played back the satellite images, and the 'boys' did the clean-up. Ty was visibly concerned when he discovered 'the whole picture'. I shook for days.

The following night, they held a huge meeting and barbeque at the fire pit outside the ranch house. It's the first time I met the other SSF team and their shooters. They each shook my hand, then stepped back, looking at me like I didn't line up with the description they had of me.

When I saw the Glow-sticks, we had quite a conversation. They put their arms around my shoulders. It was nice to have the comfort of friends who completely understood the job. After I loosened up a bit, I held my finger up as if it were a gun and pretended to blow the smoke away "Another Black Hole Crime Fighter Conquers the Bad Guys" and we all chuckled. It was childish but released a lot of tension. I wondered if the other two shooters would eventually join our 'club'.

The end result of the whole mission was that the two SSF teams were successful in eliminating the last of the pods overseas, and the team of three shot the men very active in 'the big disaster'. It gave me a feeling of relief and satisfaction. I was proud that a Canadian helped to put an end to the horrible devastation and the enemy's continued threat posed to other countries.

Chapter Eleven

The Precipitation

The last experience precipitated an extreme case of the 'floating heads'. I spent a lot of time in my upper room, existing mostly on Blue Martini because my stomach was too upset to digest food. Mary-Ann and her daughters stepped in as hostesses of the garden parties. Farmer Harry's wife, Alicia, joined in. Mary-Ann discovered Alicia was an accomplished seamstress, and started sending some finishing work her way.

Ty kept in close phone contact with me, then after a few weeks came to visit. He had been talking to a neuroscientist and brain surgeon, also very successful in treating depression with Transcranial Magnetic Stimulation (TMS). This machine zaps magnetic currents through the brain, targeting the area causing the distress. They thought it would help my condition. Ty said he had a chopper ready. The doctor was expecting us.

Ty had arranged with Dr. Sanja all of my medical history, agreeing to keep some of my true history solely in his head. Therefore, when I arrived at the hospital, the doctor was ready and waiting, going straight into treatment.

Try flying, then entering a cat scan machine, accompanied by a multitude of floating heads. I was close to hysteria. I prayed his treatment would work, and quickly. Even worse, when the doctor hooked me to the magnetic machine, he placed a hood over my skull secured by a series of 'screws' to keep me perfectly still.

Even through my haze, I could see he lacked the detached and preoccupied look that many doctors possess. His eyes were kind and his demeanor calm, voice soft and reassuring. He did a series of 'zapping', taking me to a private room between sessions. Each session was twenty minutes per day and continued over several days. Each day he would look into my eyes while examining my skull with his fingers. Sometimes I would be taken again to the cat scanner, then back to the 'zapper'. Gradually the floating heads became less frequent. When I emerged more alert, we had a talk about the side effects. There might be some memory loss, especially of the experiences causing the 'precipitation'. Since I couldn't function otherwise, loss of memory would just have to be dealt with as gracefully as possible.

When the doctor decided the treatment was successful, I was able to carry on conversations with both him and Ty. What a relief to be rid of the affliction and converse normally! I had lapses in memory, but it was mainly of any experience causing the 'problem'. Ty educated me on these subjects, so I had knowledge without feeling the personal experience. That was a good compromise; the memory without the emotion, and no 'floating heads'. Ty warned me that I may have lost my shooting skills. I assured him I was happy to retire anyway.

As follow-up treatment would continue over a long period of time, it was arranged that the doctor would have accommodations in one of the lower rooms generally occupied by the team, commuting by his own private helicopter to the hospital. He would take me with him when I required further treatment. To my surprise, he was an experienced pilot, flying with the precision in all weather conditions, expected of a brain surgeon. He was the one who delivered me home after my hospital stay.

Accompanied by Benjamin, I conducted a tour of the entire house, minus the upstairs room. However, feeling that I could trust the doctor with my private information, I described it to him.

I learned that his first name was Sanja; that he preferred to not use his last name. He liked the personal touch, which promoted trust and intimacy with his patients. He said, here at home, he preferred the family drop the 'doctor'. He was stunned by the beautiful garden and mesmerized by the moving walls. He joined the garden parties when he was home, being introduced as a family friend. I was surprised to learn that Ty and the doctor went way back.

So, my experience precipitated 'floating heads' which precipitated my complete retirement, which precipitated a rather permanent house guest. He was quiet and kind. He liked to cook Indian food, and surprisingly, he loved my mystery movies and had no problem with repeated viewings.

Chapter Twelve

On to the Next Chapter of My Life

A Fair in My Honor

Personal note: Do you do that? Whenever I have a significant change in my life or turn a new corner, I refer to it as 'the next Chapter'. Sometimes I close the door so firmly on the last one that I hardly recognize myself anymore from previous Chapters. After all, one is changed by experiences, and emerges from their cocoon a new and beautiful butterfly, or Angel, as the case applies.

Dr. Sanja called me by the name the family bestowed upon me and fit in beautifully with everyone, often accompanying Steven and Sean to Harry's to make the Blue Martini. He apparently was instrumental in forward ideas for inventions that improved production significantly. He was also very proficient at running the surveillance equipment in Ty's office. They had a background but I didn't know what it was. They kept that to themselves. The flying skills plus the surveillance involvement suggested they had worked together at some point.

The fair was the next main event. Mary-Ann made a gorgeous blue dress for me, and the hairstylist, Paul, worked his magic. This fellow also doubles as a shoemaker. He makes all of the cowboy boots for the family, and is so renowned in his work that it's not uncommon for him to ship throughout the States, and often overseas.

Until now I did not have any of his shoes. He took a mould of my foot, then presented me with white cowboy boots and a very comfortable and tasteful pair of shoes he designed specifically for 'the dress'. I was so extremely comfortable in his shoes, that from that point on I wore only 'Paul's Shoes'.

Sandra, Mary-Ann's daughter, helped me write a return speech, honoring the communities and the lovely people within.

It was a warm, wonderful day, not just the weather, but the people as well. We hugged so much that I think I became three inches skinnier and three inches taller (I wish). The school children were present, showing all the skills the Formidable Seven had taught them, including a landscape display. There was vegetable growing, pie judging, quilting displays, clothing designed by school children; and to my surprise, entirely baked, grown, and judged by the children!

The mayors made speeches, then presented me with a huge carved rabbit that would be placed in my garden. One sweet little girl in a frilly dress approached me with an equally cute black bunny with a bow around its neck. Had they heard that bunnies were my favorite creature? She asked me what I would name it. "It's a boy" she added. I held him up and looked carefully into his eyes, kissed his wiggling nose and said "I'll call you Robert."

I took Robert home that night, and accompanied by Benjamin, walked him through the entire house, including 'my upstairs room', then through the garden, giving him nibbles of various plants and flowers. His eyes glowed, and when I put him down he ran around doing 'bunny flips' in the air. He ran to the fish pond. I was afraid he would jump in and I'd have to go in wearing my pretty dress. However, he flopped down on a stone beside the water, and put one front paw in for the fish to nibble. He made a cooing sound. It's not a typical noise for a rabbit, but I would come to find out that he was a very unusual creature. This became his favorite past-time. If I couldn't find him, I would check the pond.

The next day, Wendle came with the huge carving, along with a tractor on a flatbed. He asked if there were a back way into the garden, as the item was very heavy. Before I could answer, we were surrounded by six strong men from the ranch house. The seven of them dug up plants and placed them aside to be replanted later, to clear a path. They brought the big creature in, giving it a new home near the pond. Then the plants were put back in the ground in an even more pleasing pattern than they were originally.

'My family' went back to work at the ranch house leaving Wendle and I to visit a while.

Robert jumped right up on his lap and they made friends. He tucked the bunny under his arm as I gave him a tour of the house and patio. Back on the ground floor, which was level three, we sat in wicker furniture and I offered a Blue Martini. "Oh Ma'am I don't drink" was his reply. "Neither do I" I assured him. "Blue Martini is an invention of farmer Harry, made of twenty-nine fruits, vegetables and even flowers." He took the martini glass awkwardly at first, but soon got the hang of it. He was relaxed and friendly, talking about the fair and the success of the children. He had three, he said. Then a thought crossed my mind as I walked over to the controls of the double-story living wall, turning on the garden scene. He just stared at it and didn't talk for several minutes; "it's breathtaking, simply beyond imagination."

After a little more conversation, he asked rather shyly, if I would consider accommodating his men's group from the church who meet once a month? They came a week later and I pulled out all the stops. The garden was lit, including the beautiful ever-changing fountain. I opened up level three, turned on the living wall, Steven and Sean served in their usual elegant style, Robert entertained with his bunny antics, sitting in each of their laps, eventually falling asleep on one. Around two a.m. Wendle made his way up the stairs to find me. He said he thought they had over stayed their welcome, upon which I assured him they had not. "Why don't I give you a few more bottles of Blue Martini to serve and you can party till dawn?" I suggested. What a night they had! They invited Steven and Sean to stay and party with them, so the two men rolled up their sleeves and grabbed a martini glass.

I think I developed a somewhat shady reputation as a party house. The Group of Seven hinted at it on their next visit. Well, with my usual cheeky attitude, I again hosted an all-night party, and darn, we partied till the sun rose! After we had sat in the garden for a reasonable length of time, I brought them inside to the third floor, then up the stairs to the second. They stood along the balcony as I turned on 'the wall'. At different intervals, I changed the scene until they had enjoyed everything the wall had to offer. It's the first time they had been totally silent. I just kept refreshing the blue drink. When conversation resumed, I gave my best cheeky persona "Now Dahlings, no one has had a better party than my favorite ladies!"

Chapter Thirteen

The Snowball Effect

I had started feeling like a lost lamb again, lacking the purpose of 'the job'. My last experience somehow left me feeling defeated. We came out on top, but it took so much out of me, and the treatment had obliterated some of my memory. I didn't feel the same confidence or security any more.

My seven lady-friends noticed and tried to help. Was I over-extending myself with the garden parties and other commitments in that direction? Did my new house guest put too many demands on me? I explained it away as a nervous breakdown of sorts and assured them the treatment in hospital was very successful, and I would soon regain my energy.

I spent some time alone in my upstairs room trying to think of a new 'purpose' that would make me feel fulfillment again. Sometimes when you open your mind, the right thing comes your way and you have to be receptive.

Steven and Sean had been talking for months about building a restaurant in a nearby town. It was a trendy place, where Mary-Ann had her shop. There were a few artists; a baker (Catherine), an old fashioned ice cream parlor and some other interesting businesses.

The boys wanted their restaurant to be unique, to be a place like no other, great for lunches and afternoon tea, but provide evening dining with a large dance floor, bringing in some top entertainment on weekends. They dreamed, even though they knew they didn't have the funding for such a large venture. The best thing to do is set a goal, then work toward it. They were already training two cousins as chefs in the ranch kitchen.

I liked their idea. I had been paid huge sums of money and simply banked it. There was a large payment from Ty for the years under the sea, an extremely generous bonus for restoring his thumb, huge pay cheques from the government for every mission, and the last one was just being arranged with my bank; the largest yet. I was fed for free and Mary-Ann wouldn't take any payment for the beautiful clothes she designed for me. Ty built the house as a thank-you. I simply didn't have overhead or expenses.

I made my way over to the ranch kitchen and pulled up to the counter, asking for a cappuccino. I began talking about a program I watched on television about the opulent forties and a popular night club with a floating dance floor. I imagined it as a large round hardwood floor in the middle of the room, slightly raised; with the dining room a full circle, surrounding it. Large extravagant chandeliers would light the entrance and the dance floor, with ornate sconces on the walls, dimly lighting the intimate tables. The boys joined in with their ideas, and we passed an amazing afternoon. I was getting my mojo back and sparking theirs.

I casually asked if the ranch backed onto the nearby town where Mary-Ann had her business, and would there be room for such a structure, as well as an abundant parking lot? They looked at me suspiciously, answered "yes", so I told them I'd like to talk to the family architect, Thomas, along with them, to see if I had enough put away for such an adventure. We included the accountant, Alan, who was familiar with my accounts, and a whiz at crunching numbers.

We met several times, and were presented with designs and colored drawings. The restaurant was underway.

It brought the dormant adventurers out of the woodwork. Papa's Thursday client, Harold, had been in negotiations with the ranch next to his. He thought, initially, that he would have to sell due to health issues, but decided it would be for an entirely different reason. His son had college degrees in the hotel business and loved the work. Harold could purchase land at the nearby lake, to build a resort hotel for his son.

Papa caught the wave. Hs schemed with Harold about getting out of the ranch business, sell land near the town's edge for the restaurant and other businesses, then build a golf course next to it.

The family already owned riding stables, which his wife had actually built, but when she left, they hired a riding instructor to run the small operation. Many of the town's people boarded their horses there and took riding lessons. This could be upgraded and expanded, to allow horseback riding to visitors. Sandra was already involved with the stables, participating in many riding competitions with top honors. Papa could provide his granddaughter with the business of her dreams.

Steven and Sean thought Papa should just provide the land free of charge for the restaurant, but I pointed out that if we bought it, he would not be able to 'skim off the top'. I assured them I had lots of funding for the structure from the ground up. I would be leaving my house and money to the family in my will, so they didn't have to worry about any interference from me. Once the restaurant was finished, I would write that off to the two of them.

I told them if the others came through with their ventures, it would provide the clientele they needed to make their restaurant successful. It would pick up Mary-Ann's business even more because the ladies would need appropriate evening gowns for the opulent dining experience.

I thought it was the restaurant that would snowball; but it put many other businesses on a roll too. Now that's success!

Chapter Fourteen

The Prodigal Wife Returns

Papa and his wife, Madeleine, have kept in contact by phone during the past few years, with only one visit when Papa went to Boston to visit the two sisters. In a recent conversation, he had mentioned the restaurant, hotel, golf course, and stable plans.

Well, that was his wife's stable, financed by her family's money. Papa had a way of interfering, or taking over as the case may be, and she was having none of that!

I immediately paid a visit to Mary-Ann (and Rebecca) at her shop, the main concern being for Sandra, as she was at the stables if she wasn't at school. Mary-Ann poured two coffees and took them to her bistro table. Mine always had one-quarter-coffee three-quarters-milk as Rebecca liked to sip with me.

Mary-Ann's eyes twinkled a little so I knew it was going to be good. The story was: Richard and Mary-Ann were close with Madeleine, who had actually given them the house in town, a large southern-style home with verandas running all the way around, and a yard with tall trees, complete with tree-house.

When Madeleine built the stables, Richard and his wife and two girls were able to afford magnificent jumping horses, enabling the whole family to enter competitions together. "Gee, I didn't know you were horsey. I thought it was only Sandra. I'm going to have to pay better attention." Then to Rebecca "Do you ride too?" She shook her head yes.

The story went on: The girls were born after Madeleine left, so they had occasionally gone to Boston for an evening of ballet with the girls' Grandma. She said "Madeleine's not the warm sort. The girls don't climb up on her knee, however, they sit on a chair beside her and carry on a conversation. Madeleine is dignified, classy, and may be described as majestic. She and Papa lock horns easily. He thinks he's the boss, and she knows he isn't."

She went on to tell me that Madeleine thought it would be a good move to expand the stables, sprucing it up a bit with flowers and fountains, adding more stables, training areas and jumps comparable to some of the better academies, developing it into a classy riding academy, putting it on the map as it were. "She doesn't think she'll stay, but would like Richard and Sandra to take over. The land the present stables are on is owned by her family." "Oh, so the two families had been neighbors, when Papa and Madeleine were children?" I asked. The answer was affirmative, her family still owns much of the town. "That's why she could give you the house then?" I inquired. "Exactly" Mary-Ann replied with a smile "and the business."

Much enlightened, we said our good-byes and I spent some time by the fish pond with Benjamin and Robert, contemplating the new information, and the future. I was rather nervous to meet Madeleine. She sounded slightly formidable to me; she, majestic and me, casual and friendly. I did have my friendship with Mary-Ann and Richard on my side; maybe that would help.

When Madeleine arrived a few days later, Steven called and informed me she was there, extending an invitation to meet her. I suggested that when they had time, he might bring her over to see the garden and meet me on my own ground.

In a few hours, I saw Steven, Sean and Madeleine approaching my front porch. Blue Martinis were ready for them, to enjoy as we walked through the garden. I hoped she and Ty had a good relationship because I would start with him building the house, his offices being on the lower level; then show her the ingenious moving walls and the garden. It had won everyone else over; let's hope it worked its magic on her.

We toured the upstairs; then down to the third floor. When I started the moving wall, there was complete silence. I went slowly through all the selections, with Sean refreshing our drinks. (Good, hurdle one completed, I thought).

Just then, a racing terror of black fur came from the garden, and sprang right onto Madeleine's knee. (Oh Crap, I thought, scratch hurdle one!). To my great surprise she held him up, saying "There you are Robert; and how's my little boy doing?" Kissing him on the nose, she continued "...and are you going to show Madeleine how you climb a tree?" With that they went off to the garden where he climbed the tree over the fish pond and draped himself over a branch, admiring the fish below.

Robert came back down as we began the garden tour, pointing with his nose to each and every flower in the garden, showing Madeleine the beauty of each. She talked to him in low, approving tones. She asked as we went back into the house, if I could arrange for some of these amazing plants and flowers to be planted at her stables.

Sitting down again, after the tour of the bottom three floors; the office, each guest room, as well as the equipment that conditions the air and recycles the water, she remarked "I have heard of your 'job' from which you are now retired. Yes, Ty was to visit me a few days ago. I have also heard from friends in town, and from family members, of the great work you have done in this region. I am particularly grateful to you for pointing my sons in the direction of ambitious enterprises which will be very fulfilling." She nodded toward Steve and Sean. "Steve tells me you have a shrewd business mind as well, purchasing the land, providing complete independence and control." I answered "I had a lot of time to think, three years under the ground with Ty."

She laughed "I know, he's a unique individual, but I understand you can hold your own with him, and anyone else for that matter, including the 'Formidable Seven' as you have named them. You have your own unusual style and it is working its magic on the neighborhood. You're doing good work here. You have set a lot of people straight," and lifting a martini in the air "and set a lot of people on their feet. Good work Angel."

I now have the stamp of approval from a lady who is discerning and affluent. She has good intentions toward her family which is a bit of a surprise (and relief) to me. She had not been spoken of, but now I realized they were just being discreet.

Chapter Fifteen

Dinner at the Ranch House

The dinner was formal with everyone dressed to the nines. I noticed Madeleine acted formal too, not as relaxed as she was in my garden. I suspected being in the same room as Papa had that effect on her.

The dinner was followed by music and dancing. We had a few of these dinners at the ranch house, but none so formal as this. Many of the family were musical, taking turns playing various instruments and singing. I was so very grateful to Ty for teaching me to dance. What fun! I wore the dress and shoes I'd worn at the fair which were perfect for spinning in.

Then I saw Papa bow in front of Madeleine and take her hand. He twirled her onto the dance floor. They took my breath away; smooth synchronized movements; both tall and graceful. What a wonder to watch. To my delight, they danced all night. Even though I loved dancing, I loved watching them more.

There were groups of family: brothers, sisters, cousins, abuzz with ideas for the newest developments. So-and-so could work with so-and-so. There were many offers of help in construction and landscaping. I noticed a couple of the younger cousins were school children who trained with our 'Formidable Seven'. Projects were underway.

Just when everything was going smoothly, I heard Papa's distinct voice telling Madeleine "My dear, I don't think you should have left us." Heads turned and the room went quiet.

Steve quickly piped in, "Yes Mother, you left me with Papa as an infant and look how I turned out; gay and slave in the kitchen 24/7." The room was in an uproar! Whatever Papa had tried to start was squelched; thank goodness. It was a pity to put a blue note on our absolutely perfect evening.

Papa wasn't through. He raised a glass to toast his wife and the family they had brought into the world. A sea of blue glasses were raised to the ceiling, and I felt such pride for farmer Harry. There was absolutely no alcohol being served, nothing but Blue Martini.

I heard a voice close to me; Richard. He said he was filming much of the evening, pointing to cameras mounted on two walls. "I think Harry would like a picture of this" he told me. "I was thinking that very thing" I answered. Richard went on to tell me that Harry's old home was converted to a potting shed and 'blue' distillery; a picture would look great on the wall. "I'll frame a large one" he replied. "Could you do one for me too?" I asked. He nodded in reply.

Madeleine singled me out later to tell me she was going to be a guest at a friend's home near the lake. They were travelling for a few months, and would like to have someone look after their place. We talked about the plans she had in mind for the riding stables; very impressive. The hotel would bring business to it and vice versa; everything would bring business to the restaurant. "If my husband comes through with the golf course, which he sounds positive about, each business will complement the other, making the combined endeavors a booming success." She thought a good completion date would be two years.

I asked what her opinion was of an opulent, forties themed restaurant, and she displayed great enthusiasm. "My family has some chandeliers and lights stored, as well as tables and wooden trolleys, even ceiling tile, fans and carpeting." Her parent's folks owned a large hotel back in those days. They stored many items that were just too nice to sell or give away. The occasional items have been used in their homes, but much is still available. "I'll take you to see it in storage one day, if you like" she offered. (You bet I'd like, I thought.)

*Personal note: I think it's unusual to dream of a forties night club, but a program on the history of the country triggered my imagination. I take things like that one step further; I want to **be** there. In addition to that, I've always had a love for the past; its*

91

articles and lifestyles. Hey, I'm not the only one; what's Antiques Road Show all about?

This strong interest is what draws me to the murder mysteries; Sherlock, Nero, Poirot, studying their attitudes, transportation, dress; every detail. We are purchasing more land than the restaurant requires. How about a small mall, with the same antique decorating as the restaurant, with intimate shops containing dresses of that period, and jewelry, and shoes, for the people who really want to get into the costume theme? Oh boy, I'd better not voice that idea. You know how these things catch on. We have enough on our plates as it is!

By the way, did I mention that Madeleine negotiated with her husband for the land? I thought that was the role of the architect. Kudos to the lady. She surprises me......... and how about her supplying the fixtures from her family's collection? I'm so happy about that, I could do some cartwheels. Oh now, I'm getting very silly. I must go home and get some serious sleep!

Chapter Sixteen

The Invisible Man

I slept for a while but was restless so I sat beside the fish pond with a cup of green tea. The lighting in the pond made the fish glow various tropical colors, as well as sparkling on the ever changing fountain. It was cool and restful. Robert caught my eye as he was trotting slowly down a pathway apparently chasing a bug. I don't know what alerted me, but I concentrated on the illumination of the garden plants and saw ...... yes ...... the displacement of air. I don't know how else to describe it. I calmly strolled into the house, suited up, and loaded a gun. I crept back out into the shadows and stood very still. Finally I caught sight of Robert again, still stalking someone.

I aimed and warned "Show yourself or I'll shoot." Presently, Sanja appeared. His eyes followed my voice and Robert trotted over, stopping at my feet. I continued "The only person I've seen do that is Ty; I had no idea you could too. You gave me a start." "Well," he said "you're scaring the pants off **me**. Please lower your gun and step into the light." Still rather annoyed, I retorted "I don't think you're the one to make demands here. You're in my garden, blinking in and out, scaring me into next week." He calmly walked over and took a seat by the pond.

I decided I was over-reacting at this point, went back in the house, locked my gun away, and dressed. I arrived back at the pond with two cups of green tea, my offering of peace. He said "You call it 'blinking in and out'. How do you even know about it, and further, I have never met anyone who could detect a person 'blinking'."

I explained, "Ty did it in the underground shelter. I was often just staring at the wall, when I would see displacement of air. I thought at first that my eyes were tired, but it happened often enough that I came to realize it was Ty. He had said he and his team developed senses beyond the five, so I put two and two together." Sanja asked if Ty knew I saw him. I answered negative to that.

"Angel," his voice showed concern "even the team isn't aware we can be seen. There are very few of us, to my knowledge, who can disappear from sight. Ty taught it to me years ago, then to his team. It's very valuable in certain circumstances."

"Aha" I thought, then out loud "are you a member of the SSF, or were you at one time?" He replied negative, as he followed the path of medicine, but since they were close he was aware of the SSF's 'work' and trained with them at times, including flying choppers. In his younger days they sometimes used him for surveillance or rescue work. "We've stayed close" he added.

"I wouldn't be concerned. If Robert wasn't tracking you, I don't think I would have noticed you. I only picked up on it out of repeated exposure, therefore, someone seeing it once or twice would just think what I did; tired eyes."

"You need light to see the displacement. I used the lights of the garden." I continued, "That's a good training pastime when all else is done; tracking the blinkers."

He questioned me about the gun, saying he didn't think I was involved any more. I confided that I continued shooting practice daily, although it wasn't the same, but I could still shoot accurately, at least enough to defend myself. I practiced mainly for hand/eye coordination. Shooting was something I very much enjoyed, so why stop?

Robert sat between us at the pond and pouted. Perhaps he thought he was partly responsible for the bad feelings. The doctor said he knew how to cheer him up; he had never been in the chopper. He hoisted him on one shoulder, and soon they were flying toward the sunrise on the east coast. He was able to meet up with the team, who were in the process of marking out a new mission in that region.

The doctor headed a meeting with some news that the whole group found disagreeable. They then practiced their invisibility skills; while half the group were 'blinking out', the other half tried to detect their location. They found it very frustrating until Dr. Sanja taught them to use deep meditation, staring at one spot on the wall. Sure enough, they began 'seeing the unseen'. (You have to give them credit for holding their deep concentration, with Robert tracking their foot movements across the ground).

Before Dr. Sanja and Robert headed back to the ranch, Ty asked "Has she picked up on anything else?" "I have no idea" was the answer. "I thought my job was to keep an eye on her, thinking that meant protecting her. I didn't think for a minute that I was protecting the team *from* her!" "Well, look both ways" Ty advised.

Chapter Seventeen

Research

The team had no worries, as I became preoccupied with planning and building the restaurant. I didn't conduct myself in an interfering fashion, I just sat in on meetings and enjoyed listening. It's one thing to build a restaurant. That alone is quite the undertaking. However, to make it an authentic forties structure, complete with furnishings, takes research and insight.

Our architect, Thomas, found it intriguing, as this was a completely different challenge for him. We heard there was something similar in New York, so one evening the good doctor suggested we investigate. He has rubbed elbows with some very influential people in his line of work, many of whom are very grateful, and glad to return a small favor. It was for that reason that we were able to get in the door.

Sanja met me by the outdoor pond dressed in a tux and bow tie, and I was wearing a deep blue velvet evening gown designed in the forties time period. We left in his chopper, landing on the roof of the structure, where there were four heli-pads. Escorts greeted us upon arrival, guiding us to the elevator and delivering us to the front entrance.

It was frowned upon to take pictures but I wish I could have. There were chandeliers, plush carpeting, velvet drapes, exquisite crystal and fine china. I felt a little out of my element, but Mary-Ann had given me pointers, and I followed Sanja's lead. They offered six dining choices, each twelve course, from the appetizer, antipasta, salad; ending with a flambé dessert followed by a strawberry dipped in silky chocolate. We had to compromise on the main entrée as he didn't eat beef and I didn't eat poultry. Seafood was a good choice, and brilliantly prepared.

After dinner, a swing band floated us around the dance floor for hours. I hadn't realized that Sanja was a perfect escort and an exquisite dancer. At daybreak, we were ushered back to the chopper, and home to the family, who had breakfast laid out in the dining room, even though it was four a.m.; ears waiting to hear every detail. Boy, did our forthcoming venture have something to live up to. Floating on cloud nine, I felt I would settle for nothing less!

Just before we left, cloud nine got a little jolt when Mary-Ann singled me out. She asked if the doctor and I were getting 'involved'. I told her that I noticed most of the family seemed to have chosen a single status, as marriage did not mix well with their busy lifestyles. Ty not only could not, but would not choose a relationship. The doctor was the same, with his work, and certain involvement with the team. That suited me perfectly as, I myself, just didn't mix well; as the cliché goes 'doesn't play well with others'. I found over time and experience that I was horribly miserable when I tried to share a close relationship with anyone.

I continued, "Single and free of commitment is ideal. That's one reason I'm not even actively involved in the restaurant. I'm holding back, ready to step out completely when the time is right."

She looked a little confused and offered "Dr. Sanja has family in India; a wife and four children. He married young, by an arranged marriage. However, he came here chasing his career and has never gone back. His wife did not follow him, but divorce, I surmise, was not an option." I shrugged and told her I didn't know about that, but it didn't matter to me.

Later, unwinding in the living room in my own home, the doctor and I were able to have a very frank discussion. Attribute it to lack of sleep and an almost magical evening.

I told him that I felt he was always watching me, looking for signs; but what I wasn't sure. He mused "The watcher being the watched." "I guess that's it. It's not comfortable" I replied. He opened up about his request from Ty, mostly that he was to keep me safe, with a rather tongue-in-cheek remark about 'look both ways'.

"Well Sanja," I confided, "Ty has a military attitude; not one I feel I can open up to. I am to have my shoulders squared and do my duty. Therefore, I didn't mention, well, anything actually; certainly not seeing him blinking in and out; certainly not how fearful I felt, or bored at times, or confused." He found my description of invisibility quite comical, eventually adopting the term himself.

His soft voice reassured me "Ty is the leader of the best of the best. He expects the best from himself and gets the best from others. However, Ty and I have known each other from kids in college. We grew up together so have a very different relationship than either of us has with anyone else. We discovered early on that my work with brains and neuroscience assisted effectively with his understanding of training practices, and further, just how far the human mind can bend. In addition, he is a very unique individual. Together, we amaze ourselves with our accomplishments. It's a sweet deal."

He went on "Perhaps you and I can be direct and honest with each other. You are like that just naturally so if I soften up in my communication with you, things will go much differently. Ty's question is 'What else do you see, or know?' I think there's more."

"Yes there is" I agreed. "You and Ty have advanced skills in reading people, even beyond the people I see interviewed on television. It's like Robert. He knows instinctively if I need comfort, if I'm sick, if I'm going out, when I'm coming home; which by the way it's not by the vibration of my feet on the ground; he knows **when I'm actually leaving** a place to come home. Those are highly developed senses that usually only an animal possesses. In this family's radius, it's dogs, horses, and Robert. Now, when I was on the last difficult mission prior to meeting you, the hunting dog, Benjamin, arrived at my side to guide me just at the precise time I felt I couldn't go on."

I continued "Now, when I came to the hospital for my first meeting with you, you asked me to look into your eyes, while you probed my skull with your finger tips. You used a cat scan for further diagnosis, but you knew from your physical examination exactly where the problem area was. You left me in a quiet, private room to recuperate; after a few hours repeating the physical examination of my skull. I thought that it was partly diagnosis, partly a healing touch."

"You have remarkable insight, Angel." he said with respect in his voice. "You are absolutely bang on. Let's leave our conversation here, then in a few days, talk some more; maybe things you observed about Ty. I have a feeling you may be able to enlighten me about my old friend. Let's get some rest."

I started for my room, hesitating, then turning back "One last thing. That thumb sure healed awfully quickly. Not only that, he stayed alert through what was sure to be excruciating pain, and guided me through the entire operation. That is **way** beyond remarkable."

I turned to leave, but looked around a second time "You know, Sanja, I heard wise words that stuck with me. They were from the mouth of Anderson Cooper's mother, Gloria Vanderbilt "I am not here to see through you; I am here to see you through." With that, I left.

Dressing for bed I had another thought. I put on my bath robe and went back to the living room. I was glad to see the doctor was still there. "Sanja, there is something else on my mind."

"Mary-Ann stopped me before we came home, asking if we were getting involved. I told her 'no' and that I don't have a problem with that, as I'm very happy to be free and clear of involvement of any sort. Then she said you were married by an arranged marriage in India. You never speak of your family, and I'm curious."

He sighed and his answer astounded me. He said his mother had come to him one day, saying he was very gifted; at the top of his field and rising, but a very bad husband and father. "She realized that I had to put all of my focus on my work as a surgeon; that was what I was meant to do in this life. She knew my wife was miserable in the marriage, but loved the children. Her family was wealthy and could help her raise the four babies."

He continued, "Honestly, Angel, I didn't even know my family. I was never there! So, with my mother's knowledge, I went to the U.S. for a conference, not intending to return. As it happened, at the same time a plane went down, taking the lives of some of the passengers. With Ty's help, my name was put on the passenger list. That left my wife free, after a period of time, to marry if she wished. She married ten years ago, and Mother assures me he is a very devoted husband and father. I'm very happy that things turned out well. I speak to Mother and Father every day, often from the hospital. We have a good relationship and there are no hard feelings. I legally changed my name, went back to university to further my education, and receive status in the U.S. as a surgeon; and the rest you see."

He added "I was not happy living in the city. I was very much alone, except for my involvement with Ty's team. After I treated you, Ty saw I was lonely and suggested I move here, where there is some family activity. I already owned the helicopter, which is most convenient. I love flying."

He continued, "Your home is intriguing and beautiful, with an amazing garden in which to unwind and meditate. I hope you don't mind my presence here. I try to give you your own space as much as I feel you desire, and I know you have your private room if you want to be left alone."

I told him I found his story amazing and touching. He had sacrificed much for the happiness of his family, and his own sanity. I was very satisfied with his 'intuition' of my need for privacy, and I had no problem with him making his home here for as long as he wanted. I would keep his information private.

He lived on the lower level, which Ty built for his team. It was ideal. It had beautiful bedrooms with moving walls, and a creative lounge area. He was not at all in my way, and he was becoming a trusted friend.

I crawled into bed and slept for hours, waking the next morning to feel my world had been set straight.

Chapter Eighteen

The Town's Abuzz

I mentioned in a previous Chapter that the work had begun. It had. The first step is talking about the ideas, working out availability of land, establishing financing, and designing the new structures.

We have now come to the next step, breaking ground, installing power and sewer lines, digging basements, pouring concrete, making streets and parking lots where required, and so on.

Accounting Services: One of the most remarkable people was Papa. I thought he would be a thorn in the otherwise well greased wheel. Not so. Not so at all. He handed the responsibilities of each business over to his sons. Two cousins joined the team of accountants, and began services for the businesses as well as the new ventures.

The Golf Course: Papa sold off cattle and other ranch business, including sections of land for new developments, surveyed the parameters of his golf course, got out there on his landscaping equipment, and took his time carving out a marvelous course, planting trees and flowers, installing fountains. He enlisted help for the club house, but the rest was all his own work. It took him about four years, and he enjoyed every single day of it. He looked forward to doing the maintenance himself, once the course opened. He was a different man, and was using his given name, Anthony, the new image taking fifteen years off his appearance.

The Hotel: His Thursday client, Harold, brought his son, Arthur, home from the hotel he was managing in the city. Together they sold the ranch to their neighbor, then used the money to purchase beach side land at the lake and started pricing building material for their resort hotel. They eventually hired Thomas to design the structure, incorporating some of the restaurant ideas into their lobby and some of the theme rooms. It started as a relaxed lake-side holiday refuge, but they caught the wave and went with 'resort with elegance'.

Some lake-side owners were disgruntled about a twelve story hotel invading their landscape, so meetings were held with Thomas present, and they worked together on a compromise. It would instead extend backwards, making it six stories. The rooms would be built around a courtyard complete with outdoor swimming pool, swim-up bar, Jacuzzi, wading pool with fountain for the kiddies, and free passes to the facilities for all of the nearby lake front owners. Peace was made. Palm trees would surround the hotel and bright-colored tropical flowers would add to the ambiance. With the kiddies' facilities in the courtyard, the beach front could be a more formal design, complete with circular driveway and valet parking.

The Stables: Sandra and her father worked with Madeleine on the stables and riding academy. They came up with innovative designs that change the jumps by remote. There are walk-through horse baths, and exercise machines to assist with warm-ups. There is a delivery system to the stalls, making feeding efficient, and conveyor belts for easy clean-up. The end result is pristine living quarters for the animals.

Various riding rings provide access to training on varying levels. The main jumping arena has a concession stand, and covered bleachers. There are spectators all day long, to watch their children's lessons, to attend show jumping competitions, and comfortable seating for participants to relax between events.

Chapter Nineteen

The Restaurant

We involved Madeleine as a consultant, mainly for decorating the restaurant. We investigated her family's stash of décor from the forties, finding two chandeliers of slightly different design, eight feet in diameter, made of crystal and gold. One was perfect for wowing people at the grand entrance, and the second adding elegance to the circular floating dance floor in the centre of the dining area.

Thomas set to work on the elaborate entrance. The room was square, but a circular design in the floor made it appear round. The chandelier hung from a domed ceiling, with ornate moldings around the fixture itself and around the base of the dome. Two corners were perfect for the placement of washrooms; the doors hidden behind large white pedestals, draped with huge ferns. The other two corners were for the reception desk and coat check.

Once the floating floor was installed, Thomas decided he liked the domed ceiling in the entrance so well that he installed the same over the dance floor. He protected the floor with a tarp, then cut a hole in the roof with supports for the large fixture. He used pearlescent paint, with accents of deep blue and vibrant gold to accentuate the colors of the dining room. The result was breathtaking.

Steven and Sean decided against a lounge as such, but accommodated a subtle one by placing small rectangular tables around the perimeter of the dance floor. On the outside of these tables, they placed a ring of large round dining tables with small ornate lamps on each. All tables and lamps were a generous donation of Madeleine. A very wide aisle between the rows of tables was covered with plush carpet in rich gold and deep blue, reflecting the colors in the ceiling. This aisle would allow the maitre d' to parade the guests, showing off their beautiful evening gowns.

Thomas' creative juices were flowing. He carved out a geometric design in a circular pattern below the entrance chandelier about fourteen feet in diameter, then poured molten gold into it. He was enjoying himself so much that he repeated it on the dance floor. He had an audience. We all held our breath as he poured the extremely hot metal, but he pulled it off without error. He bowed and we clapped.

The kitchen was out of sight to the patrons, so Thomas was able to bring in the best in modern equipment. Following the shape of the dining room, the kitchen was built in a crescent shape, allowing easy movement of the chefs and prep staff. It was clever and magnificent!

Actually, the whole restaurant was magnificent, including the design of the steps up to the entrance doors which, Thomas couldn't resist, adding a little gold inlay there as well.

The ceiling was very high. On the walls of the dining room were tall, narrow tinted glass windows, dressed in deep blue velvet drapes with champagne colored sheers, pooling at the floor. Beautiful sconces were placed between each window. Some modern design was, at times, combined with antique, but in a very tasteful way. Second to none, I was sure. It would put all guests on cloud nine for an evening of dining and entertainment.

We put our heads together and came up with the name WISTERIA. It seemed to give the feeling of 'the 'past' and 'fine dining'. The sign was placed on the front of the building in pale lights; variegated colors. You have to see it to really appreciate it.

Steve and Sean (now sole owners) held a pre-opening night, with all family and friends in attendance. They actually hired Josh Groban to entertain for that evening, and again for opening night to the public. I almost stumbled when I saw Papa, now Anthony, at the reception desk as their Maitre d'. While everyone was milling about, I had the chance to comment to him in the voice of an 'upper crust' "Anthony, you seem to be moonlighting. Is the golf course so expensive you have to supplement your income?" He gave his best dignified look and the voice of the family butler in movies. "Madam, my sons agreed to let me hang out here so I could meet all the famous clientele. In return they will provide a meal for me at the end of the day. I may also impress friends here on my days off, free of charge" and then cleared his throat.

They managed top billings for every Friday and Saturday night. The entertainment shared the evening with a local swing band, often joined by talented family members on trumpets and saxs. They were a class act. The afternoon teas were serenaded by harpsichord. It may sound extravagant, but with Madeleine's donations for practically all of the décor, and Thomas' innovative thriftiness, the restaurant came in way under budget. I left the spare funds in Steven and Sean's hands to have some fun with.

The boys adapted the menu from the forties restaurant in New York; offering four choices, each twelve course, varying the preparation of the entree. The choices were beef or pork, poultry, fish, and seafood. It was a very popular dining decision. Instead of the strawberry dipped in chocolate, though, was a dessert cart with 'Catherine's delicacies'.

The boys were able to charge well for their dinners, especially when their guests saw what the dining experience offered. There were certainly no complaints. It brought in many celebrities and government officials, as well as foreign dignitaries. This increased Mary-Ann's business, expanding her designs to famous ladies throughout the U.S. and sometimes, foreign countries.

Thomas adopted some ideas found in my garden to decorate the grounds, and throughout the parking lot. We made use of all the land we had purchased. We found a way to eliminate parking valets. It was very unusual. Each vehicle was parked between vegetation and tropical flowers, illuminated by feature lighting. The guests walked through an imaginative and uniquely lit garden to the front entrance. It even made parking a talked about event. We found the locals residing only a couple of blocks away, were bringing their cars, just for the parking experience.

I still held my garden parties every Friday night, but came to the restaurant nearly every Saturday. One evening, to my extreme surprise, Ty graced the entrance with his mother on his arm. They stayed until closing. I was very impressed, and so, apparently, was he.

Soon after he arrived, he slid in beside me for a moment and in a low voice "About that 'blinking' as you call it; were you ever going to tell me?" "No" I answered. He replied, "I'm a little perturbed about that. I want my money back." I looked at him straight on and smugly said "Spent it" waving my hands to indicate the restaurant. He answered with a wink, and went back to his evening.

Dr. Sanja, who was very busy, couldn't attend opening night so when he had a Saturday night free, he asked me to accompany him to Wisteria, adding that it was only fitting we attend together as we had 'researched' the restaurant in New York. I hadn't told him a thing about the new restaurant, so I was anxious to see his reaction.

He was very quiet, examining every detail with his eyes; driving very slowly into the parking lot, taking his time through the garden, up to the front door, examining the railing, stairs and signage; through the entrance, where he stood for a few minutes just inside the door. His reaction to Anthony was priceless.

We were escorted down the wide circular aisle then seated at a quiet, well spaced table. He looked around for a long time, completely silent. We were served Blue Martini in exquisite goblets. He sipped, then turned to me and said "I have to apologize for taking you to such a dump in New York." I smirked back and replied, "I forgive you. The food was good, and the transportation unique." He kept Saturday nights free after that. He couldn't pry himself away, once he had the 'experience'. I was happy about that, as he was a dream to dance with.

Chapter Twenty

The Hotel Experience

I wasn't sure how I'd react around water, but decided it was time to spend a week at the resort hotel. I hoped the floating heads wouldn't appear again.

I chose a more quiet time, booked into a lakeside view theme room, (Egyptian), why not? They had a good reputation for their daily buffets, and weekend brunches. I borrowed one of the family cars and set off for the lake. Mary-Ann was going to host the garden parties.

Close to the destination, there was a look-out which provided a picturesque view of the lake and hotel. What a magnificent place! They had hauled in white sand for the beach, the water was clear and blue, the hotel was surrounded with palms and ferns, accompanied by bright tropical flowers. From my vantage point, I could see the swimming pool shaped in a whirling design, swim-up bar, heart shaped Jacuzzi, kiddies wading pool and fountain with some sort of floating ride going around in a circle. Everything on the pool deck was painted a pale blue with darker accents. The front of the hotel was all glass, curved, with a completely circular driveway. A flower bed, fountain and palms decorated the centre of the circle. The building itself was made of some material that looked like white sand. It oozed of total elegance.

I drove down a winding hill and pulled up to the front door where two valets met me, one taking my luggage, and the other sweeping back down the drive to park my car.

At the front desk, Arthur met me with a smile and handshake. He sent the bags to my room so he could give me a grand tour of the hotel and beach. The windows in the guest rooms were slanted to view the lake, a design feature meant to provide privacy to nearby homes. They were staggered so as not to impede anyone's view. The rooms opened with French doors onto balconies, the size for standing only; the kind I had seen in pictures of Italian architecture.

The top floor had a lounge, with comfortable blue sofas and pale blue Indian carpeting; the curved glass window gave a view over the lake. The buffet and Sunday brunch rooms were on the main floor, decorated in a tropical style, greens and florals. (They, of course, had dessert choices fresh daily from Catherine's bakery. Someone is always available to take a trip out here early in the day). Every room, including the lobby, gave the atmosphere of a breezy lakeside vacation; no problem getting into the mood here!

His tour included the mechanics of the structure. It was run exclusively on solar power; everything, including the kitchen equipment and air conditioning. The air cleaner was unique (no wonder the air felt so fresh). He pointed out cleverly hidden vents along the baseboards and walls of every room, including the restaurants. The system extended to the lobby, effectively cleaning every particle of air. An ingenious design, the vents near the floor had stronger suction, pulling dirt from shoes and clothing. I had an even greater respect for Thomas' professional skills and imagination.

Arthur then directed me to a second, smaller lobby at the side of the hotel where guests could come and go to the beach. Great feature; no wonder the main lobby was so pristine.

We walked to the water, leaving by the secondary lobby. Arthur told me they had ordered oversized umbrellas in different pastel colors with swirling patterns, to be placed along the beach. It was another of Thomas' clever inventions. He had already drilled holes and implanted long poles with a ball mechanism on top, barely showing above the sand. He pointed out the flags marking each one. When the umbrellas arrive, they will be fastened to the poles, one edge resting on the beach. The ball feature will allow patrons to roll the umbrellas in all directions, shading them from the sun at any angle.

Arthur gave me an earful as we splashed along the water's edge, explaining the exotic design and many expensive innovations of the hotel. The conversation included their attachment to Anthony. Arthur's mother had passed away when he was in the first grade. He and his father from that day on became 'partners'; Arthur calling his father by his first name, Harold. The young son had become 'a man' in a hurry and they worked hard, but the ranch was falling apart and so were they.

Papa, seeing what was happening to his neighbors, took the situation under his wing and put them both on their feet. A monetary reward was involved, but father and son didn't complain, as they were both lost souls without his help. Papa made sure the son got a good college education in his choice field, hotel management.

This brings his story to the present, the hotel. Keeping his hand in things, Papa helped with the sale of the ranch, all paper work involved, also arrangements for the new property. He continued to do much of the bookkeeping, delegating some of the tasks to the accountants in his family. He knew Harold was a good worker, but not experienced in business. Arthur returned home, father and son began plans for their new project, at which point Papa sent Thomas over to assist; ensuring it would be a place of beauty and success. When it came to the expensive pool deck, Papa paid a visit, returning every penny he charged over the years for keeping the ranch on its feet. With Thomas' help and the extra funds, the hotel was their dream beyond dreams, and their pride of a lifetime.

I told Arthur I had the impression that Papa was a bit hard-nosed and not inclined to kindness. I had been told he was poor in relationships but controlled his 'ship' with great success; putting his sons in lucrative businesses, charging each of them for his involvement. Arthur said he was indeed like that for many years. He had to be focused and stern to make his family a success. He was a formidable foe in business transactions. That trait was what saved their ranch from falling victim to pressure from the next rancher over, who was hungry to claim more land at the cost of his neighbors who were hurting to keep their heads above water. The subsequent sale was slightly above the going rate. Papa too, knew how to deal with a hungry buyer.

However, recent events gave Papa a new perspective. He realized he could loosen up, trusting his sons were completely capable of running their own lives. He had a meeting with the whole group of boys, telling them he was a good businessman, and that the running of the ranch (and a good nest egg) was paid for completely by his success. Therefore, he was able to pay back every penny he had charged to run their businesses.

The process of selling his neighbor's ranch, and seeing Arthur and Harry into a new venture, gave him insight into such a change bringing great happiness. Papa came to realize he would love to do the same. "He's a changed man" Arthur said with emotion.

118

Following suit, he sold portions of his ranch, began constructing his golf course, saying it was the journey, not the destination. Anthony's sons hardly recognized him, but it was in a very pleasant way.

"You know" said Arthur, "Anthony put every bit of the proceeds from the sale of the land back into the restaurant, paying for most of that innovative, modern kitchen." I gasped "I am so surprised!   No wonder the money stretched so far. Thomas said it was because he was thrifty." "He is" replied Arthur, "but we all received a leg up. I think it was influenced by his respect for Thomas' skills and thriftiness, and Alan's diligence with accounting and taxes."

Later that evening, Harold and Anthony came to my door with a trolly laid out with a dinner for three, including candles. They said it was better to dine privately as the dining room was packed. I had noticed during the day there seemed to be an awful lot of people milling about. I commented that I thought I was coming at a quiet time. The answer was that they booked me in when they had an opening for a theme room. That was their best rendition of a 'quiet time', as their hotel had become an overnight success. Locals, and visitors from abroad, all booked much in advance.

When my company left, I fell into bed exhausted, but had trouble falling asleep, with the conversations of the day running through my brain.   I kept all information private, as I thought that was the unspoken agreement.   If Anthony wanted anyone to know his business, including the restaurant venture, he would talk about it himself.

Chapter Twenty-One

Weekend at the Hotel

Sanja called me at my Egyptian room. He told me he was keeping a better eye on me since I had 'surprised his socks off' over the restaurant business. He said Ty had a twinkle when they met last, but didn't let on as to what it was about. He did, however, comment that Sanja was not good at guarding my safety. I told Sanja that when you are all work and no play, there is much of life you miss.

He told me a new surgeon had joined their team at the hospital, enabling him to have a little more time away. Sanja then asked if I would mind company for the weekend. He thought I had a knack for finding new adventures. He had talked to Arthur and found there was a plain room available for a couple of days. I answered "Sanja, it's like Wonderland; nothing is as you expect it to be. Plain will be anything but."

By the time he arrived by chopper, the umbrellas were in place on the beach, rolling gently in the breeze, making it an even more amazing experience. Seeing the hotel for the first time by air was even more spectacular. He hovered for quite a while before landing.

When he eventually knocked at my door, he whacked me over the head with his hotel reservation calling me a "Smart Ass". "Smart

Ass! Smart Ass from the doctor?" I teased. "First Wisteria, then the hotel; I nearly flew the chopper into the lake. At least you told me the plain room wouldn't be plain. It's so impressive!" he answered. I chuckled "How easily impressed you are, my friend. Wait until you see the Egyptian room!" He walked around the room, examining every feature, decoration, and ornament; shooting me the occasional nasty glance. I was rolling on the floor laughing. My poor dear friend didn't take surprises well. In all his brilliance he could still not keep up to me.

"Want to get even more surprised?" I queried, "I'll take you on a little tour." He stood in front of me with his hands on his hips, trying to look foreboding "It was a fast trip, as Arthur was busy, but he took me around, understanding that you would be too sassy if you were allowed the privilege." I acted like a Smart Ass anyway (sure suited me better than Angel) "Awh common sour puss, let's hit the beach. Do you know how to sail? They don't allow speed boats on their pristine water, but a neighbor has offered his sail boat, as he's away this weekend." With his usual competence, he maneuvered the boat around the amazingly clear, blue lake. I had no idea a sail boat was so luxurious and so very impressive. This time it was my turn to be surprised.

Sanja asked Arthur if swimming in the lake was accepted. "Later in the evening" was his recommendation "and with a spotter." Arthur offered to row alongside, in a canoe. They pulled an all-nighter, taking turns rowing or swimming. You would think they would be exhausted, but arrived for breakfast refreshed. Thereafter, they continued their practice, Sanja swooping down in his chopper after work on a week night, often at a late hour, and out the two went. Eventually, Sanja convinced Harold and Arthur to install an endless pool on the deck. They compromised and placed it on a deck at the rear of the hotel, as it had to be enclosed and locked, for safety reasons. It allowed one to swim against a smooth, adjustable current, even flexible for water jogging. Sanja paid for the pool himself.

There is so much to tell you about the hotel, which by the way, they named 'LUXURY ON THE LAKEFRONT'. It would take a

Chapter just to recall to you a day on the beach, or a day on the pool deck. I hope to write about some of this in the future on repeat visits, but I'll end with a description of the Egyptian Room.

The door itself is made of a solid stone slab, carved with Egyptian drawings. The handle is a replica of an ancient artifact. The opening of the door activates sounds of a fountain and birds singing. A section of wall is a 'moving wall' showing a bath scene with a fountain, and 'Egyptians' walking around or bathing.

The floor of the entire suite and bath are white marble. The bath is ground level with steps leading down into it. An Egyptian lady is lying beside the tub, pouring water into the bath when a lever is moved. Fresh rose petals are in a dish on one corner so you can sprinkle them into the water. Large urns are placed around the tub and throughout the room. On top of the towels are jeweled ankle bracelets and arm jewelry, if you really want to get in the mood.

The bed is held by 'slaves' carrying royalty along the streets, complete with wonderful Egyptian cotton sheets, and curtains that can be pulled aside. A button on the wall activates a moving palm branch to fan you while you sleep.

Throughout the room, chairs are shaped like mythical characters, some with moving eyes. French doors open onto a small balcony providing a picturesque view of the lake. Wine is in decanters of that era, with jeweled goblets, for your enjoyment. (I poured some out and found I was provided with Blue Martini).

Pleasant Dreams.

Chapter Twenty-Two

Golf on the Range

That's correct, Anthony used a play on words to name his new golf course GOLF ON THE RANGE. The club house was now finished, chef in place, practicing entrées, inviting tasters from the town to help him decide on a popular menu. Steven was occasionally consulted.

Honoring many requests from Anthony's friends, once the front nine was finished, business began, while he proceeded to work on the back nine. He found it helpful, as there were a few very valuable suggestions from seasoned golfers who said they would like to see this or that on the course.

The golf pro was very involved on the back nine, as this part of the course had to be designed with more difficulty, including longer, curving fairways, and challenging sand and water traps. The putting greens must not disappoint. The pro hit ball after ball, making adjustments until he was satisfied. Richard made himself available two days a week. He would play through the front nine, honing up his skills, then join them for the rest of the day, often running the ball catcher on the driving range, or in the early hours, mowing the grass on the front nine. The rest of his time was spent at the riding academy, which was his first love.

One Friday night at the garden party, the Formidable Seven made arrangements for me to join them at the course the following Monday, since the course now had a golf pro to teach beginners, and give lessons to seasoned golfers. Most of us seemed to have swing disabilities, but eventually caught on, even if our methods were a little unconventional. One couldn't see the ball in flight, one couldn't find the ball if she were standing on it, one couldn't drive the cart, and so on. In the end, with combined skills, we saw each other through the games, which were to become a regular Monday event.

One Monday, Mary-Ann asked if I would look after Rebecca as it was a 'teacher's day'. I took her with me to the course, rather than find another activity to occupy her for the day. Well, that beautiful little child, now eight, could hold her own in a conversation on any subject with her seniors, plus she had a wicked golf swing. She became our newest member, giving up the occasional morning at school to join us on the fairway. Her mother was a little surprised, but actually pleased that she had branched out in her interests.

Mary-Ann was now working flat out, with the orders for 'forties style gowns' made expressly for evenings at Wisteria, along with her regular work, as well as the children's clothing line. She hired Harry's wife Alicia full time, and two of the Formidable Seven part time, so we were not concerned when they didn't show up at the range. They were great with dress designs, and expert with hand sewing, lace collars, and covered buttons; indispensable talents.

Harold came by many weeknights to golf the front nine with Anthony, after the last team had played through. Often Anthony would snag the chopper if it wasn't in use, flying Harold back to the hotel. The pair would wander down the beach until sun-up, when the next work day would resume. Robert often accompanied them, chasing down the beach after gulls, sometimes charging back to Papa to release a freshwater crab from his nose.

The men's church group, having their fill of the garden, took to the range. They doubled their numbers, solved problems expediently with fewer personality clashes; and had the golf pro take minutes of the meeting, while stopping occasionally to adjust someone's swing. The minutes would sometimes include "... Paul sliced again, in spite of all the hours of lessons." The larger church issues, they would put on hold until they had the full eighteen holes to ponder the solutions. The pro wanted to know if this meant he was now a member of their church.

Anthony, while working away on his landscaping and tweaking his sprinkler systems, formulated a design for a whole new kind of golf cart, solar powered. When Thomas had time, they put their heads together and the end result was awesome. It was a sleek design, turned on a dime and held a single person. It had a bottle holder that cooled the water, a rack at the back for the clubs, an umbrella, which would be designed for, and provided with the vehicle, also a compartment for accessories such as a jacket, balls, and score pads. They later decided to provide the jackets as well, with the name of the golf course on the back.

Anthony ordered golf clubs and carts for each of his boys and surprised Harold with the same. He took his jacket home to wear around the hotel. He was so very proud.

Chapter Twenty-Three

The Kentucky Derby Knock-Off

Madeleine, Richard, Mary-Ann and girls had met many people at competitions over the past few years, some of which expressed interest in attending a small competition at Madeleine's riding academy.

It came to the point of giving the stables a proper name, so they came up with COUNTRY MEADOWS RIDING ACADEMY.

The long weekend was approaching so Madeleine got together with some trainers and riders to make a decision to host an event next year on this date. It meant a lot of planning and as usual, the situation grew and grew.

For accommodations, they thought a ring of A-frame cabins surrounding a camp kitchen would be a nice touch. Each cabin would have a front porch, with two rocking chairs. They could also build small gazebos near the cabins, providing tables with shelter for the visitors. The final count was thirty cabins (just in case). The guests would be asked to supply their own bedding and towels. A small kitchen counter would be installed, with a coffee maker; nothing more since there would be a breakfast buffet. Thomas also wanted to build the beds himself, as they could be custom designed to fit the cabin, and of sturdy construction.

Thomas had a lot of experience at this point building kitchens, so he thought, why go small? A large structure in the centre of the circle could be erected, housing a large, modern kitchen, with attached laundry facilities that could be shared with the guests. He had such success with solar power that he preferred to go that way again. It would power the large kitchen, lights, water heaters in the cabins, as well as the yard lights. Water and sewer would have to be installed; construction to begin immediately. They could bring water up from the canyon, tapping into the line running to the ranch house. A separate water filtering system would be necessary.

The next concern was for more stables. The accommodations at the riding academy were more than adequate for the 'regulars' so expansion would seem undesirable, However, the ranch barns were quiet now, making them an obvious choice for visitors.

Roadways were the next concern. They would have to cut through the ranchland because the towns couldn't accommodate horse trailers, and the expanded traffic the event would generate.

The grandstand, they decided was well designed and built large enough to accommodate any visitors who came.

"Thomas, now that we have discussed possible future plans I need to talk to Anthony" said Madeleine. "It will affect him enormously. There is much land required for the cabins, as we are giving each one a lot of space, and the roadways will cut through the land. We will have to park horse trailers somewhere out of sight."

"There will be a lot of traffic, people and animals milling about. We will have to draw a plan so he can see the impact it will have on the ranch, on him, and on his golf course. It has to be laid out so it's not visible to his course or the restaurant. It would be bad for the businesses already in place, and for the town as well."

Thomas reminded her that since they weren't divorced, the land was just as much hers. She replied "Yes, Thomas, I know what you're saying, but it's been a verbal agreement from the beginning that the stables are mine, and the ranch is his. Our word is our honor. If he feels it will be an unwise move for the ranch and the family, I will respect his decision without reservation."

"By the way," Madeleine explained, "your father made no plans without talking to me first, not for my approval, but out of respect."

Madeleine went on "We may not see eye to eye, but we know we can trust each other completely. That is the basis for any friendship, and that is how your father and I have stayed friends over the years. It is also the reason our family is close. Above all else, we trust and love each other."

Thomas and Madeleine paid Anthony a visit a week later at the ranch house, and discussed the proposal over a candle light dinner prepared by the cousins now running the kitchen. They later cleared the table, making space for the plans Thomas had drawn up. "Anthony," Madeleine spoke softly "this is just a little idea I had that came out of requests from fellow competitors. The little idea expanded into possible plans for a very large expansion. I really don't want to change our riding academy, as such, but it would be fun for myself, Richard, Sandra and Rebecca to bring some big names into our small town to have a little fun together. People seem to crave the country atmosphere, which beyond a competition, would be a small holiday."

Anthony thought some roads could be adjusted, but otherwise found the plans quite agreeable. He wanted an additional road to lead from the ranch house to the golf course making his trip to work a lot more convenient. It would also encourage visitors to the course. He then pointed to some symbols, asking what each meant. One was for solar panels, the other for water filtering. When he queried if it could be expanded to service the ranch house and barns as well, Thomas replied affirmative. When Thomas thought they had the thing all tied up, Anthony rolled up the plans, saying he'd like a few days to look them over.

Thomas jumped up and charged out the door. When he got into his truck and turned the ignition, he looked over and jumped, as though he had seen a ghost. Anthony was comfortably seated beside him. "What? How?" was all he could utter. Anthony replied "Well Thomas, if you're going to roar off down the road and over a cliff somewhere, I'd prefer to be with you. However, it might be better for our health if you just told me what is on your mind." Instead, Thomas put the vehicle in gear and started down the road. Nothing was said for miles and he drove as fast as he dared. Finally, an hour and a half later, he pulled into the look-out over the lake and hotel.

"Papa, I'm just so disappointed. I did a lot of detailed work and planning, even making colored drawings of the cabins, fountains, and all other landscaping. Then just when I think you're satisfied, you roll up the plans, indicating you're not with us on this."

Anthony put his hand on his son's shoulder "I'm sorry I gave you that impression. It's just that I've had my attention on the golf course for months, making it hard to wrap my head around the riding academy plans. I'm thrilled, as I am with all your work. Your mother has a great sense of what she likes, and when she likes it, it's always good. I just need to take a couple of days off the l andscaping machines, to concentrate on your proposal of the academy. I see some things there that may be good for the course, as well as the ranch house. You just keep getting more imaginative with each piece of work you do."

Anthony went on "Thomas, you are a gifted architect and designer, and I feel I hardly need to question any of your work. You rise above and beyond anyone's expectations. I can't wait to see what you come up with here. I just want to be able to understand and appreciate your every step. I'm with you; oh you bet I am! I want to enjoy it too. I promise no interference; maybe a request here and there for the golf course or the ranch, but that's all. Some features are intriguing." Thomas backed the truck up, and headed back home.

While driving he said "Papa, I have to apologize; I acted very foolishly. I'm rather wound up lately. Elizabeth broke it off with me because I haven't spent much time with her. I bought a ring and was planning to propose. Now look; she's dating Alex - a rich bastard the next county over."

Anthony replied "You know the lesson from your mother and I. You must have also observed Richard's relationship with his wife and family. Whatever you're doing, no matter how important it is, no matter how much pressure people are putting on you, your personal life must come first. How rich is the bastard, anyway?" "Oh, I don't know, a few million or so" he replied. Anthony gave his son a hard look, "Thomas, did you count your assets, son? I put all your contributions back into your account; it's not pennies. You've earned a whole pile more with your recent work – the hotel, the golf course, the restaurant, the clubhouse, the academy ….."

Thomas glanced over "Papa, that's family. You don't charge family." Anthony snorted "We are all very lucky to have your work. It's a cut above anyone else's. You deserve every penny you earn. The family has all set aside their fee to you, including me. When I was talking to the accountants, they said the customers are asking them for their bill. I thought they had talked to you." Thomas replied "Well, they did mention something, but I just ignored it, thinking they were just talking."

Anthony smiled "Son, you're worth at least a billion. Drop me off at home to talk to Madeleine. Knowing her, she's sitting there patiently, knowing I'll return. Then for goodness sake, take the ring over to Elizabeth and propose. Then arrange with her regular dates, and have her come to the ranch house for breakfast every morning, before you both start your day. From now on, put her and yourself first."

Sure enough, Madeleine was right where he left her, three and a half hours earlier. "A little misunderstanding, it's okay now." He joined her in dessert. When they were done and sipping their coffee, "Madeleine, my dear, are you investing your family's money, or do you want to use some of our own family's reserve?" Madeleine replied that she had plenty of funds, and this was for **their** family anyway. "Using Angel's example, at a certain point, it will all be transferred to Richard, Sandra and Rebecca's names." "And you'll pay Thomas generously?" he asked. "Most generously!" she replied, then "Are you billing me for your land?" A very emphatic "No!" from Anthony "It's your land as much as it's mine."

They received a phone call an hour later telling them that Thomas and Elizabeth were now engaged, and would like a party on the weekend.

When construction was underway for the academy, the Formidable Seven approached Mary-Ann at a Friday night garden party. They thought it would be 'a hoot' to make the event a mini Kentucky Derby. The men could wear their best suits, the women could dust off their party dresses, make elaborate hats, and show their visitors they were a fun and classy bunch.

They also thought it would be nice to involve the school children from all four towns. It would give the marching bands a chance to entertain, and the choirs to combine their talents for a great stage show; perhaps a musical.

They could also order fancy stemmed acrylic glasses, serve wine to adults, and punch to the children. It would show the children how to attend a formal function with the adults.

The following Friday, Madeleine made an appearance at the garden party, exchanging ideas with the ladies. She was touched that they wanted to make it such a grand affair. They calculated attendance, deciding that a second grandstand would have to be built on the other side of the show jumping arena to accommodate everyone comfortably. In honor of their sophisticated guests, the grandstands would be painted a clean white, and white stones would decorate the walkways. Potted flowers would have to be brought in as well. To Madeleine's great surprise, the ladies told her they intended to pay for all of the upgrades, including the second grandstand. The Formidable Seven had struck again.

Chapter Twenty-Four

A New Friend

That Saturday night, I was getting ready to go to Wisteria when Robert came in acting very anxious. He stood at the bedroom door, just looking at me. When I approached him, he turned around, heading down the stairs to the third floor walkout. I followed, by this time feeling anxious too. We went out through the garden and past the back gate. There I found Benjamin whimpering over something and licking it. I thought at first it was him who was injured, but as I approached I saw it was another animal; closer, and I could see it was a dog, skinny, beaten, and near death.

I phoned right away to the kitchen who in turn called for help. Soon there were two men carrying the poor creature to the ranch house for treatment. As they were working on him, inserting an intravenous, cleaning his wounds and assessing his condition, Anthony came rushing through the door. He did what he could, then said "No one around here would do this to an animal. It has to be those crazy coots down in the canyon. There has been the occasional person killed in this area too, but no one was found responsible. I have a strong feeling they were involved." He looked at me and explained "There are three brothers as far as I know, camped down there. They have a lean-to and distillery. They're drunk all the time. This poor dog looks like their work. Our surveillance doesn't go into the canyon, so we can't see what they're up to."

Then to his sons "I'm going to get a small lens and plant it in a tree, pointing it at their back yard. One son followed him upstairs, to help locate the surveillance equipment he wanted. When they returned, he grabbed a rifle and headed out the front door. "Wait Anthony" I called after him "it doesn't sound like a one man job. Come down to the house with me. It's getting dark so I can suit up. I have three guns that shoot quite a distance. They will be better than that bulky rifle."

He waited on the porch and I came back in full suit, with the guns. "I'll put the rifle in the kitchen and give you one of these nice babies. It shoots eight bullets and gives no flash." I had to run to keep up, along the edge of the canyon, then down a steep path towards the bottom. It was a long hard hike and he had to help me most of the way. He was very steady on his feet; I could tell he was used to this path.

When we reached the bottom, we went along a rough trail, eventually getting close to their camp. Anthony instructed me to get close to one of the large trees and stand very still, watching for movement. He said they were a crafty bunch and could very well be hiding out, with rifles aimed. I could see one of them sitting on a stump near the cabin, tending a fire. I looked around but couldn't see Anthony, so I held my position, alert and listening. He was right. The other two had to be close by, ready to shoot.

I waited, but nothing was happening, so I trained my eyes on the one man. Sure enough, I could detect displacement of air circling around him. (What the heck? Was that whole family born with the same gift; invisibility?) Presently the man sensed something and began looking agitated. He finally looked very definitely to one spot in the woods, then to another spot not far from me.

Next, the man ran into the cabin, probably to get a weapon, and the 'blinker' followed. I knew he wouldn't be coming back out. Another few minutes passed, then a shot rang out from beside me. I edged my way over, looking for movement. I started when I saw him right next to me, looking straight at me, realizing I was there. I made a loud hiss to scare him; his eyes opened wide with fright. Pop and he was silenced. After another long pause, the next man crept cautiously out of the trees, circling around toward the cabin. Pop and down he went. Anthony appeared in the cabin door. I waited, afraid there would be another shot, but the air was silent.

Finally Anthony walked over to a tree, climbed it, and planted his camera. He then came toward me saying "Thanks Angel; excellent back-up. There was no other way. I'm going to do a little staging, retrieving your bullets, and shooting them in the same spot with their own rifles. I'll make it look like they shot each other. I hid a camera in case of more activity here; just a precaution. It's well hidden. No one will ever detect it. The community will now be safe."

I stood in the darkness of the tree, keeping my pistol aimed in case I needed it, but all was silent, except for the two bullets Anthony put into the dead men.

We made the long climb up the canyon wall, Anthony pulling me most of the way.

When we returned to the ranch house, there was a little movement in the new patient. Dr. Sanja was there as well. He was expecting to accompany me to the restaurant, but our plans had changed. He was placing his hands gently on the dog, helping to heal his wounds. In a few hours, they removed the intravenous, so I filled a small bowl with the blue juice and started splashing it around his mouth. Soon he was lapping it up and looking for more. Robert kept close to his face, cooing to him, and Benjamin laid beside him, comforting him. It was a miracle for sure, but he lived. We gave him the name Freddie. It just seemed to suit him.

Freddie was able to hobble within the week, eating alongside Benjamin and Robert. His hair gradually grew in. He was black and white, and wiry with long legs. He had a limp, and had trouble getting up once he laid down for a rest. It was hilarious. Robert would push his way under him, starting at Freddie's head, so that only a fluffy tail showed under his chin, then Robert would lift up, until Freddie could get a grip with his paws.

In time, he lost most of his limp, and unceremoniously got to his feet if Robert wasn't there to help. I personally think the Blue Martini did its magic as well. I gave him a martini glass twice a day. He looked at me with those soft pampered eyes, knowing he was very spoiled, and grateful to his rescuers, mainly Robert and Benjamin. I don't know how they got him out of the canyon in that condition and to my back yard. They're very special little animals. Thanks to them, we have a new friend, Freddie.

Chapter Twenty-Five

The Engagement Party

Thomas and Elizabeth got together with family members to plan an extravagant party. They decided it would be nice to serve the appetizer at the cocktail party leading up to the dinner. Once seated, she would like a butter lettuce/avocado salad with mandarins and slivered almonds. A seafood soup would follow. The main course would be sole rolled around stuffing with a white sauce, and the dessert would be one of Catherine's creations.

Steven and Sean approached her carefully with their desire to present engagement rings to each other that evening as well. She was delighted with the suggestion. She even helped them pick out their rings.

When Anthony got wind of it, he bought gold necklaces to present to the boys, as they couldn't wear the rings while cooking, understanding they would like to keep their precious rings close.

He then got together with Madeleine to decide on Thomas and Elizabeth's engagement gift. Madeleine thought wine glasses and a decanter from her family's collection would be treasured.

Unknown to her, Anthony and sons agreed to present a family ring to Madeleine that evening as a token of their appreciation and love they have, no matter where she decides to reside.

It was Elizabeth's suggestion that the sons give a huge diamond ring to their father as well. He was responsible for ensuring they all had lucrative business, and unknown to them over the years, had saved all of their contributions, recently giving them a large monetary gift along with full ownership of their companies.

Thomas was not sure how Elizabeth would take the big 'ring giving' evening but she was bubbling over with excitement. The girl he nearly lost was going to be a wonderful and caring asset to the whole family. He didn't know her folks well, as they lived in Hawai'i (native spelling, which her family uses), but anyone raising such a daughter must be the best.

I was concerned for Elizabeth. In this family, everyone just stepped in, putting their own spin on things (to put it delicately) so I invited her to the garden one evening for an intimate conversation. It was hard to talk to her because she was dashing about, discovering the moving walls, the garden, and other creative features. I think the Blue Martini finally calmed her down a bit, so we managed to settle out by the fish pond with Robert, Benjamin, and Freddie. I'm going to have to give them a name – Trio something. I asked Elizabeth about the 'ring' celebrations, even having to plan it for Sunday, as Friday and Saturday were already taken.

She told me she was an only child, growing up in Hawai'i, then came to the States to attend university. She was studying architecture, meeting Thomas in one of the classes. She settled in a nearby town once they graduated.

She gradually met his father and brothers, and came to appreciate that Thomas came from an exceptional family. She said they had hit a little 'bump', but was grateful to Anthony for straightening them out. She was extremely happy to join such a wonderful group of people. They made her feel like she belonged.

I asked if she was working in architecture. She found this humorous and replied "No, I have a jewelry business across from Mary-Ann's shop. My parents are jewelers and are happy I have a degree, but were even more pleased to set me up in a business in town. I make some of my own jewelry, and they ship some of their creations to me from Hawai'i. A lot of Mary-Ann's customers come to me for pieces to match their new dresses."

She went on "My parents flew over and are staying for a couple of days at Luxury on the Lakefront, before arriving here on Sunday, to stay with Madeleine. They're coming back for the mini Kentucky Derby next year. My father owns some Arabians and they both ride; not competitions, just for leisure."

Well, that took care of any of my worries. I asked if she was designing forties style jewelry, and she replied that she had a whole cabinet full of the real thing. I was **definitely** going to call on her next week; then to Mary-Ann's to have her design a dress to match the jewelry.

Sunday came and the celebrations began with a combined buffet for breakfast, brunch and lunch. The 'boys' transformed the room for an elegant evening of dining. They installed a stunning chandelier over the dining room table, and complementary sconces on the walls. Harry was very busy, producing Blue Martini for the whole celebration. No one even mentioned champagne.

Anthony started the dinner off with an elegant speech about his family and Elizabeth's family, giving insight into each other's lives. Steven and Sean closed Wisteria for the day and helped in the kitchen to produce a dinner I will always remember. The table was laid in crystal, including dinnerware (from Mary-Ann's collection); it simply sparkled and took your breath away. There were blue roses in crystal vases placed along the table to match the Blue Martini served all evening. Elizabeth's parents glowed with happiness. They also mentioned when they left in the wee hours of the morning, that they felt more refreshed than when they came. Kudos to Harry!

When we went into the main room for the dance afterwards, I gasped. Thomas saw my expression and strolled up beside me with Elizabeth on his arm. "I redesigned things with the help of my fiancée; making use of her skills as a fellow architect. We've been working on it for weeks. We installed a curved staircase going up either side of the room and knocked out some of the upstairs rooms, completely transforming this portion of the house. The hardwood flooring was there, but needed refinishing. Some of the lighting came from Mother's collection. We had to order the sofas and chairs in addition to more light fixtures. Neither of my parents saw it until it was complete. When I unveiled it Friday night for the first time, they danced around the room with no music. I guess they approve!"

By this time, some of the brothers picked up instruments. They had played every Sunday night after dinner as the family was growing up and they sounded like heaven. Elizabeth and Thomas started the dance, then went to the stage to make a formal announcement of their engagement, and gave the date for their wedding, six months away. Madeleine and Anthony presented their gift, followed by her parents, presenting them with matching gold necklaces, with inset rubies.

Next, the sons gathered in the centre of the floor, while Anthony presented the family ring to Madeleine. I've never seen her act so emotional. It obviously meant a lot to her.

Following that, Steve and Sean took the centre of the room. They were dressed in crisp white pants and shirts. They surprised everyone by reciting wedding vows, performed by Anthony, and presented rings to each other. Madeleine and Anthony then gave their gifts, the necklaces, to the two men, kissing them each on the cheek.

I looked over at Elizabeth. She had her hands clasped together with tears rolling down her cheeks. She considered it the best engagement party that anyone could ever have, with the whole family demonstrating their love for each other.

When midnight struck, the music paused, the sons took the middle of the room again, and presented Anthony with a ten karat diamond ring (one karat for each son), accompanied by a ceremony in which each individual spoke, telling how their father affected each as an individual. He cried so hard they had to usher him to his office to regain his composure. (I think a glass of whisky was poured as well).

The celebrations continued, and Sanja arrived, gliding me around the floor in his usual exquisite style that I had become used to.

At two a.m. finger foods were brought out and the celebrations continued until four a.m. We hated to break it up, but many had to be on the road again by six, and someone had to run the bakery items out to the hotel. It was back to business as usual.

Chapter Twenty-Six

The Wedding Changes Everything!

In a few days, Thomas was out at the A-frame site, just walking around where he found Yvonne out there doing the same. She was perusing landscaping possibilities, with a set of plans rolled under her arm. She told Thomas that she wanted to involve the school children, for both building and grounds.

In chatting with her, he mentioned it would be nice to have some of the cabins finished before the wedding, as they would be good guest houses. If he met his ideal, he said, he would like a finished site with a couple more rows of cabins behind the first row. She didn't say anything, her eyes just changed. She marched forward, put the megaphone to her lips, and he heard "Step it up there boys, get ready for two more rows, delivery time six months". She came back to Thomas "I can get the kids here after school for a second shift, but you need to find another competent crew for the night shift." In answer to his startled look, she replied "We need three shifts. The yard lights are up and running so we'll have night lights, plus we can tap into those for individual lights on each cabin. You need to arrange to lay out the additional plumbing immediately." Off she went. Thomas didn't know who put her in charge, but he was going to send a big bouquet to them when he found out.

This time Thomas' eyes changed. He sprinted to the truck, bypassing Madeleine, straight to
Anthony. He flew out of his truck, leaving the door open, and across to the back nine, jumping up onto the machine Papa was maneuvering. He sat down beside him, relaying the most recent event. Anthony replied "Oh ya, they seemed to need a supervisor out there so I asked her if she might be able to help." Thomas made a mental note to have flowers delivered to the clubhouse in the morning.

Then Anthony's eyes changed. He turned off the motor, "Come on Thomas, no time to waste, let's get on the backhoes to dig trenches for the plumbing. You need to get on the phone and order more pipes. Will the solar panels put out enough power?" Thomas sat there for a moment "Is it just me, or has everyone lost their marbles?" then "no, we're all nuts" and off he went.

By the time the plumbing was installed for two more rows of cabins, Thomas had revised his plans, making larger cabins on the second and third rows, adding two more bedrooms and two bathrooms. He phoned around and found a place where he could buy A-frames premade; perfect. That would make the proposed finish date a reality.

When the first row was completely finished, Papa turned up with a cement mixer, pouring sidewalks leading from the cabins to the large kitchen, continuing on to the entrance of the academy. It resembled a huge wheel. I came out to watch the day he was pouring; it was pure white cement. The time was six p.m., and the school kids were there, all ages, male and female. Yvonne had the younger ones following behind the cement truck, kneeling on the ground, inserting flat white stones of different sizes. Myrtle came behind with a flat stick, ensuring they were flush with the cement. What an effect!

I saw some flatbeds pulling up with pine trees and other shrubs. One truck was hauling bright flowers, daisies, baby's breath and marigolds. An auger had begun drilling holes, and a tree planting machine was coming in from the back, so as not to disturb the newly laid sidewalks.

The teachers had been great, compacting the school lessons where possible, to allow the children the experience of a lifetime - constructing a small village from the ground up. Most teachers rushed over after school with the children, to pitch in, erecting cabin after cabin, taking time here and there to share a laugh with their friends.

"It's a beehive of activity" I thought to myself. "I'd better clear out. I'm not partial to bees." It was Friday so preparations for the garden party had to be attended to. It looked like everyone was at the construction site, but I still had quite a few of my regulars.

We were all very appreciative of the peace and quiet the garden offered.

Madeleine came in on Mary-Ann's arm, both looking a little frazzled. She said "I just found out today that I have a much larger enterprise than I was originally expecting. I hadn't checked on it in a few weeks, but when I saw all those trees, I wondered how they would fit around the cabins. Well, it was a shock when I found out, and even more so when I saw Anthony out there hammering nails!"

"The sidewalks are beautiful" I replied, not acknowledging her plight. She looked at me with disbelief as I handed her a Blue Martini. I continued "I was out there earlier, watching the children decorating the sidewalks by hand. The effect was beautiful, but I thought it looked like a hornet's nest and retreated." Madeleine then caught the twinkle in my eye and started to laugh. She got the giggles. Whenever she looked at me, she started laughing again. It went on all evening. It gave everyone the giggles. I finally said "This is half your fault Madeleine; the boys are half yours. Does the 'crazy' come from your side, or Anthony's side? I just want to know where to sit during the wedding." I didn't get an answer; she just kept laughing. I guess the cabins were going to be all right with her; you just need a little humor to get through things. From what I saw, it was going to be a gorgeous finished product. Knowing how things began, and then expanded, I thought

154

she might eventually find it useful to the riding academy.

The wedding came quickly. The ceremony was held at Wisteria. The tables had originally been laid out so spaciously that it was easy to bring in more to accommodate the guests. Some of the food was prepared at the ranch kitchen, and the rest at the restaurant.

The opulent nostalgia of Wisteria provided a perfect setting for the wedding. The guests, awed by the garden leading to the front door, walked in silently like one does into a cathedral, just looking around, stunned by the beauty. Soft music was playing on a grand piano, joined later with stringed instruments and horns for the dance portion of the evening. The wedding party made the full circle on the wide aisle between the rows of tables before mounting the dance floor for the ceremony.

Elizabeth was escorted by both her mother and father, and Thomas was joined by both parents as well, putting all tradition aside. The bride was breathtaking in a gown handed down through her family. It was a cream color, adorned with pearls, jewels and lace. Her hair was a loose cascade of curls, intertwined with ribbons and flowers. Thomas looked like he was going to pop with pride.

After the vows, we sat down to a dinner very similar to the meal served at their engagement party. She liked to keep things simple. She told me if guests weren't stuffed with heavy food, they could enjoy mingling and dancing more. Instead of lengthy speeches, they had movies of their lives playing on monitors on the walls between the drapes.

The guests were abuzz about the beautiful country-atmosphere accommodations, and the sidewalks that had a rustic look, but poured smooth to accommodate high heeled shoes. Thomas had hung chandeliers from the A-frame of the ceilings, contrasting their rustic design. The sofas were brocade; the bathrooms, marble. He called his new architectural design 'chic country'.

The guests who chose to stay at Luxury on the Lakefront, had to take a detour to see the charming cabins, the final result being nothing short of awesome. The entrance was through an arbor of ivy and flowers. White sidewalks lead the way to rows of cabins of increasing size, adorned with a variety of pine trees of varying heights. The grounds were illuminated with lighted fountains of changing colors surrounded by shrubs.

Those who hadn't been to the hotel, heard about it from other guests; they made plans to holiday there soon. Anthony had some brochures that he discreetly handed to the guests, and brochures were on the coffee tables in the cabins. He was very proud to promote the wonderful holiday hotel that his son had designed. He made a mental note to arrange with Madeleine for brochures of the riding academy as well. That event was only six months off.

Chapter Twenty-Seven

Tying Up Lose Ends

Madeleine and Anthony met for breakfast the next morning to discuss the final phase of the riding academy. Madeleine expressed her concern over further construction as she could not have riding lessons disrupted, or activity close to the training or riding rings that would spook the horses. Therefore, it would all have to be carried out at night. Anthony suggested he pour the same sidewalks he had done for the cabins, as the competition was going to be a dress-up affair and women would be in heels.

He and Richard called in the night crew, and they laid forms for the sidewalks first. Since the school children could not be used this time, the men, along with Richard, Sandra and Madeleine, got down on their knees, laying down white stones as the cement was being poured, followed by Yvonne using a flat stick to ensure everything was perfectly level. Next, they painted the existing grandstand in sections, so as not to interfere with the activity of the daily routines. Whenever Sandra had some free time, she was right in the middle of construction, enthusiasm bubbling out all over. It kept the men in line and motivated. Then the second grandstand was constructed and painted, all at night.

Finally, the work was done, flower beds, fountains, and evergreens all in place. It was nice to have the work completed much ahead of schedule, as all focus could be on horses and competitors. Against the backdrop of white, Country Meadows Riding Academy was very impressive.

Madeleine's friends returned home, so she took up residence in one of the larger cabins. In the end, she loved the A-frames in their chic-country design. Thomas had paid for the second two rows, knowing it would be left to the girls. She felt renewed. She loved walking down the pathway in the morning before the lessons began. The corners of her mouth twitched as she admired the inlaid stones, remembering the garden party. She could easily get the giggles all over again. She often sat in the bleachers at night, looking out over the jumping ring. Sometimes she would be joined by Sandra and Rebecca, sitting on either side of her, placing their heads on her shoulders. They were full of pride, admiring their legacy.

Having seen the project through to the end, Anthony called the Golf Pro, making arrangements to finally finish the back nine. They were to meet at six a.m. at the clubhouse. Anthony came up the back way and around the corner to enter the building. A sign jumped out at him 'Grand Opening'. Inside he found a room full of ardent golfers, all dressed in their finest apparel, ready for a round of eighteen holes. They had joined together with the pro and finished the last of the work, making it ready for his return. All business had shut down for the day, making it possible for golfers, both men and women, to initiate the newly opened course.

After a celebratory drink of champagne, Anthony and the pro were up first, whizzing down to the first hole in their fancy new golf carts. The Formidable Seven and I got on the fairway around two p.m. when the pro was available to guide us through the newest part of the course. Madeleine and Rebecca were included in our group. What fun we had!

That evening, Wisteria put on a dinner for all. They again added extra tables they had stored after the wedding celebration. As before, they joined efforts with the boys at the ranch house to prepare an elegant meal of Steak Neptune. Before the dance began, the Mayor announced that this would be a holiday each year, named after the golf course. Anthony was very touched. While he was planning weddings and grandstands, the town was planning a great surprise for him. What an honor!

Thomas and Elizabeth called the next morning to congratulate Anthony. They had gone home with her parents to Hawai'i for their honeymoon. They said they would be gone for an extended length of time, so turn away further business for a few months. If everything went well, they would be returning with 'a baby on the way'.

Madeleine had been having breakfast at the ranch house. She asked what Thomas had to say. Anthony replied "He says they're having an extended honeymoon. I think they'll be returning in twenty-seven months with three babies." Madeleine poured the rest of her coffee in his lap and stomped out the door. One of the cousins had just rounded the door with fresh coffee, made an about face, returning to the kitchen to call Richard. He replied "That happened all the time when we were kids. Maybe it means they're getting back together."

By the time he hung up, Anthony was standing at the counter, clean pants, and an empty coffee cup, asking for a refill. "From now on boys, if you value your jobs here, anything you see or hear will be kept private. If you have a comment, say it to me. Who was that you were talking to?" When he was told, he asked what Richard's comment was. He went out the door laughing "That's my son." Thereafter, he would start his day and end his day in the kitchen, having coffee with the boys, getting to know them, and gaining their confidence. They had so much fun that one would ask Anthony to sample a new dish, saying "Please Suh, you no likee don't throw in my lap". In answer, Anthony would hop that counter like a deer, getting him in a wrestler's grip and rub whatever was handy on his face.

When he left the ranch house, he came over my way for a conversation, which was a rare event. He told me that Dr. Sanja had put a bid in for some land behind the group of cabins, saying he wanted it for a runway and hangars. I offered, "He told me he was bidding on a small learjet. I asked him what he was going to do with it and he told me 'to fly places very fast'. It was the kind of comment that squelches any further conversation. Why are you coming to me about it?" The reply, "I didn't want to ask questions. I was hoping you had the answers, but apparently you are just as much in the dark." "Well," I said "the next best person to get discreet answers from is Ty." I went on, "I would think that anything close to the academy would be undesirable; maybe at the far end of the ranchland, if it doesn't interfere with your neighbor, with an east/west approach."

"Well," replied Anthony with a grin "Madeleine just poured coffee in my lap at breakfast. Maybe an approach over the stables would be good. What do you think?" "I think" I grinned back "you'd better apologize for whatever it is **she thinks** you did, and let Sanja buy land in the next county. You're a hard nose, but your wife is a formidable foe." He chuckled as he closed the door behind him.

Chapter Twenty-Eight

The Town is Threatened

A few weeks went by smoothly, when Madeleine started receiving phone calls from the town's people; Mary-Ann, Catherine, the family accountants, and some private residents with some complaints about the mayor. She had heard that he was a pretty good mayor, but had some bad ethics. It was apparent that he planned to fatten his pockets, claiming it would be for upgrades to the town, but he had to be dreaming if he thought anyone would buy into it. His wife left him a few weeks ago and Madeleine wondered if he had become unstable as of late.

Some of the land belonged to the town, but the majority of the businesses were on land owned by her. The residents said they had received letters from the Mayor's office, doubling their taxes. The Mayor, accompanied by a well-muscled man with an obvious pistol under his jacket, was visiting all of the businesses on Main Street and adjoining streets, delivering tax notices by hand. "Honestly," she thought "are we back in the wild west?"

Madeleine, conferred with Anthony, then requested they ask for a town meeting to discuss tax rates. On the following Wednesday evening, many gathered around a conference table waiting for the Mayor to arrive. He came in half an hour late with his bodyguard in tow. He opened a file and started talking to them in a threatening manner. Just as he felt the people were cowering, Madeleine walked through the door, sat down, placed a file on the table in front of her and opened it. The room fell silent.

The bodyguard backed up to the door, blocking their only exit.

Madeleine handed a bundle to the person next to her, who passed it on until it was placed in front of the Mayor. "You're messing with the wrong town here, Mr. Mayor. You seem to be forgetting who owns most of it. The land not owned by my family is owned by the town's people, not you. The package I have handed you is a copy of the deeds to the land, and a set of by-laws, signed by you when you were elected, outlining your duties to the town, and the oath you took when elected ten years ago. I should not have to remind you of any of this. Have you lost sight of your obligation to the people?"

The Mayor lifted a finger to his bodyguard who began reaching for his pistol. He felt cold metal against his left ear. Mary-Ann swung around in her chair, and removed the gun from the man's holster and handed it to the man standing behind him. He was handcuffed and pulled backwards.

While Richard held him in custody, Anthony appeared in the doorway with his gun pointed at the Mayor's forehead. "You seemed to have forgotten, Mr. Mayor, that I am the Chief Deputy and reserve all rights to place you, and your friend here, under arrest. You will be tried in the next county. Since they are aware of the situation here, I would not expect any leniency."

Before the Mayor could get to his feet, his head was pushed into the boardroom table. He was cuffed and led away to a waiting van driven by the Sheriff of the next county. The two men would be locked up, where they would stand trial.

I put the safety back on my gun. The mayor hadn't even noticed me sitting next to him at the table.

The town's newspaper had been alerted about the meeting, and the photographer and reporter were waiting outside the door, taking pictures of the men in handcuffs. They asked for comments, but received none that could be printed. Anthony, Richard, Madeleine and Mary-Ann then posed for pictures. The photographer then took pictures of the complete group around the conference table. Madeleine presented the reporter with a typewritten copy, giving a complete report of the misadventure from beginning to end, including a copy of the deeds to the land, and town by-laws. It was going to be a big fat juicy paper this time, and the two men rushed back to their office, working all night on the biggest sensation the town had experienced in decades.

As expected, the town was unsettled over the next few days, wondering who could run for their next mayor. There were a couple of volunteers, but no one that seemed to have good qualifications.

Madeleine let things simmer down a bit, then called a meeting right on Main Street. The people tied balloons to the street lamps, had hot dog stands, cotton candy, and beverages.

They started the evening with a marching band the full length of Main Street.

A flatbed had been hauled in as a make-shift stage, lights set up, and a microphone that could be heard for three blocks. She started the meeting by giving a brief rendition of recent events, introducing the two candidates, giving an outline of their credentials and character.

She then presented a third. She told the people that she had been in close contact with the son holding law degrees from a respected university. He had enjoyed long-haul trucking over the past few years, but was ready to park his truck permanently, in order to offer his services as their new Mayor, if elected.

Mary-Ann then gave a speech, outlining his degrees, his character strengths, and his dedication as a family man. It wasn't really that necessary, as the town all knew Will, and enjoyed visiting him at the bakery whenever he was in town

The three men then gave their speeches.

The people were invited to vote for one of the three candidates at polling booths set up in the Mayor's office conference room.

The votes were tallied and the new Mayor announced at ten p.m. Will had won by a landslide. The two other candidates were the first to shake his hand, saying they voted for him themselves. "Well, I'm going to need two good men. I think our town can afford you both, so how about joining me as Public Relations, and Promotions Representatives?" They were both thrilled, so following his acceptance speech, his first job as Mayor was to announce his two right-hand men.

Will was swamped with calls over the next two weeks, and answered each one, even if he had to call them back late at night. When people settled down a bit, he put an ad in the newspaper announcing there would be an open house every Saturday from nine to six in the Mayor's conference room. He would serve coffee and cookies. It gave everyone the chance to have a voice. He had his two right-hand men attend, with instructions to treat each individual as though they were the most important person in the town.

With his time better managed, he was able to scrutinize the books which were very poorly kept, bring them up to date, then have a printout of the financial statement available to all Saturday visitors, saying they could expect updates monthly. The family accountants volunteered their services each month. They had to freeze the former Mayor's account, to retrieve the town's assets.

With the help of his two right-hand men, their next mission was to reach out to the three nearby towns by first befriending their mayors. As of late, relations had fallen by the wayside. Once they got to know the three Mayors well enough, they invited them to attend their open-house Saturdays. Seeing the examples of financial statements and open-house policy, the Mayors approached Will, asking for his help in getting them organized and approachable in their own towns. Will invited them for regular weekly meetings at Wisteria, treating them to lunch and preparing guidelines for his style of 'business'. Soon, all four towns were running by similar rules and ethics, strengthening the bond between them.

Next thing they knew, the Formidable Seven were seen with a group of school children from all four towns, working together in landscaping, and making any repairs needed to both the town's streets and private homes. They had learned so much more, creating the town of A-frames next to the riding academy.

Chapter Twenty-Nine

Dr. Sanja Retires

Things went along smoothly until one morning, while I was enjoying a cup of coffee out on the deck, admiring the ranch house. They had made quite a few changes to the exterior. I looked to the sky to see a small plane coming in very fast. It banked, then went down a few miles to the north. Maybe I should have called to see if someone might need help, but I just sat there sipping. There were no flames in that direction, so they must have made a smooth landing in a field.

I poured another cup, and sipped. About a half an hour later, a small blue sports car came down the highway, turning in to the ranch house then past it up to my front door. Sanja emerged, waved, then presently appeared in the arched doorway. I just waited for him to start the conversation.

"Did you see the learjet come by?" he asked. "Yup" I replied "and I saw the sports car pull up to the front door. My first thought was that the doctor must be going through his second childhood." He retorted "Can't possibly be. I never had the first one. "You mean you went straight into medicine at the age of six?" I asked.

Deciding he would not engage further in this childish banter, he went on "The new surgeon at the hospital has proved to be very gifted, so I decided it would be a good opportunity for me to retire. I handed in my resignation a month ago."

I didn't comment, so he went on "I tried purchasing land from Anthony for a runway and hangers, but at first he wasn't forthcoming, so I talked to the next rancher over. He was terribly money hungry. When Anthony got wind of it, he agreed to a large strip on the far end of the ranch, accommodating a long runway and hangers for the plane, with additional hangars for any future planes."

"So you can fly places very fast!" I retorted. He poured a cup of coffee and sat down. "I deserve this. I promised a long time ago to change my approach of communication with you, and I let you down. I apologize. I'll start again with direct and honest."

He sipped his coffee and began again. "I brought a colleague into the hospital because I wanted to pursue a new lifestyle. He worked out very well, so I gave my resignation. In the meantime, I placed a bid on an awesome learjet with a compartment that held this sports car you see here. I wanted the whole package. Eventually, the fellow agreed to a rather exorbitant price but it was perfect, so I purchased it."

He went on "I want three things. First, I want to have more time to work with farmer Harry on the Blue Martini, plus I want to build a very large greenhouse alongside his farm which will grow the plants needed for the product, under protective cover. Second, I want to be able to fly anywhere in the world, contracting my services out to the SSF. When the car is removed, seats flip up to accommodate the team. Third, I want to holiday." He had my attention.

He continued "Ty arranged for the government to install the runway, hangars, and fueling tank placed below the ground. I consider it good payment for my services to them."

Finally I spoke, "When did you learn to fly the jet?" He explained that he had some previous experience, plus he took lessons from the former owner. He caught on very quickly, but continued flying with him until it came naturally. That's what he was doing over the past month while the runway was under construction. Sanja made the first two landings here with the former owner before he took over completely. They had logged a lot of time, landing at several airstrips throughout the world, familiarizing him with different runways. "The fellow is a former fighter pilot. He has a lot of friends, therefore access to private runways. Honoring my involvement with the SSF, I was granted the same privilege."

He smiled and continued "I have my first mission. I am leaving tonight to pick up the team, to transport them to another destination."

He continued, "When I return home I'm hoping you will accompany me on a flight to Cuba. Have you been there?" I replied negative; the only places I had been were the Bahamas and Vegas. "Then it's a good choice" he said. "I can only stay for five days, as I have to return for another mission. I'll make our trip from Sunday to Friday, returning for your regular garden party. After that, I will be bringing Thomas and Elizabeth back home."

Mary-Ann scrambled to make a wardrobe for Cuba, mostly sun dresses and shorts. Paul made sandals. I already had shoes and dresses for evening wear. Why make more when the existing ones were so perfect? Sunday came quickly, and I was whisked off to the waiting plane in the blue sports car, driving right into the plane's cavity. We took off down the long runway and up into the clouds. I caught a glimpse of where I knew Canada to be and a feeling of sickness came over me. I looked the other way and tried to compose myself. Sanja reached over and placed his finger tips on my skull where 'the problem' was and it calmed me.

We talked about Cuba and what our accommodations were going to be. In a short time we landed on a private air strip, jumped into the sports car and went speeding off down their very rough roads to the resort. It didn't compare in luxury to the hotel at home, but it was oddly very wonderful; the relaxed and laid back atmosphere on the ocean front. Sanja thoughtfully packed some Blue Martini for me which I very much appreciated.

We lounged on the beach, splashed in the waves, body-surfed, danced at an outdoor night club in the evenings to an island beat, and shopped at the market. I got a tan and Sanja just got darker. "The Glowsticks would be very envious of you right now" I commented. He replied "Oh, I forgot. I was to say hello to the 'Black Hole'. It sounds rather rude. Does it make sense to you?"

"Oh yes," I replied; then I told him about Angel and the Glowsticks turning into the 'Black Hole Crime Fighters' and how we thought it would make a good comic book. He laughed and laughed. Time went by too quickly but he promised there would be more trips in the future.

Chapter Thirty

Thomas and Elizabeth Come Home

Mary-Ann was able to contact the former Mayor's wife, Sylvia, by phone who had already heard about recent events through friends. She was so devastated by life with her husband that she felt she needed to settle elsewhere and make a new life. She asked a neighbor to sell everything in the house, as she had taken any personal belonging with her when she left town. The rest was just painful reminders.

Will called Sylvia about legal matters, mainly of their bank account which had to be frozen. As far as he could see, her husband had frittered away the money, and what was left belonged to the town. It didn't cover everything, but they agreed at a meeting they wouldn't sue, as the burden would fall on her shoulders.

With Thomas coming home soon, he thought the large home of the former Mayor would be a good place to settle until they could build their own place. He had appraisals done of the neighbors' homes and of Sylvia's, and sent the package to her. They settled on a price, and she was very relieved to have that burden off her shoulders. Again, the town agreed to let the full amount of the sale go to Sylvia. Will then advised her to get an immediate divorce.

The Formidable Seven went to the house and cleaned it up. With the help of family members, they knocked out walls, rewired parts of the home, replaced the cupboards and deck, poured new sidewalks and replaced some windows. Once it was painted in modern colors, the home was very attractive in an open-concept style. When Thomas outgrew his need for the home, it would be easy to turn around at a profit. At least for now, they had a place to call their own in a convenient location.

Sanja parked a family car at the hangar when he left to pick up Thomas, so he would have a vehicle large enough to accommodate them.

The family was waiting on the front veranda of the ranch house when they drove up. First, Thomas emerged, waved, then bent over into the back seat to pick up his package, twins, one under each arm. Sanja opened the front passenger door to help Elizabeth out. She had a month old baby in her arms. Anthony had been completely accurate; twenty-seven months, three babies.

I saw Madeleine's arm reach behind Anthony and he jumped, then grinned. If I didn't know better, I'd think she pinched him. They then went down to the car together to meet their new grandchildren; three absolute cuties.

Richard grinned at Mary-Ann. They had talked to Thomas and Elizabeth, so they already knew; in about a month's time Mary-Ann would be making an announcement as well. For the time being, though, the information would be kept quiet.

When they were back in the ranch house, seated in the living room, bouncing babies back and forth between the family members, I saw the concern on Madeleine's face. She sat down next to Elizabeth, and asked how she was going to manage; had she made arrangements with someone in town to help?

Thomas leaned across and answered "Mother, we have learned some lessons from you and Papa. You gave him children and looked after them every morning, turning them over to Papa when you went to the stables for the day. He joyfully bounced us on his knee while he went on about his ranch business; then we were yours again from supper on. The only time you got together was over dinner, with very little communication, as you both had babies on your knee. He went back to work in his office until the early hours of the morning to catch a couple of hours sleep. I'm not sure when you found time to make more babies."

Madeleine cut in "Thomas, you know I love you very much, but I had become seriously depressed after having Steven, so your father and I both agreed that I must stay with my sister. Any time I thought of returning, I became depressed again. I seemed to have no choice but to stay in Boston. I felt terrible guilt, but I knew my husband was very happy in raising you boys; so happy it seemed, that he had no use for me anymore."

Thomas answered "We're adults now Mother. We get the full picture and harbor no hard feelings. We've all kept in close touch over the years. My point is, we are not about to make the same mistake. I talked to Richard about the design of the new house in town, and had him install a large office with two desks and two drafting tables. We won't work any time soon, but when we do it will be a joint effort."

It was Elizabeth's turn to speak "Madeleine, my uncle who has been running the jewelry store in town is very popular and doing well. The town seems to love him. I have no need to go back to it any time soon; maybe years. I don't require any outside help at home as Thomas is just as active in raising the babies as I am. We love our family life, campouts in the back yard, picnics, the playground; and we can even go the hotel at the lake. We're not poor. We can afford to raise our family together. Then when they're in school, we can resume some of our work. By the way, I doubt we'll have more than just the three."

Madeleine was so relieved that she had to walk in the garden while she digested the information. I joined her after a while, asking her how she managed with ten, one after the other. She said, instead of breakfast, she made a vegetable casserole and the kids kneeled on chairs at the counter to eat while she made sandwiches, plain meat that they could walk around eating without making a mess. I laughed so hard! When I regained my composure, I told her about the sandwiches Richard demonstrated in Canada and I continued to make for Ty.

She said "Oh my gosh! I've raised a family of sandwich-eating boys! I wonder if Elizabeth will break the cycle. Somehow, I doubt it. The boys think it's the only way food should be served."

I asked her about the vegetable casserole and how it was made. She explained it, and it sounded delicious. I suggested we collect some food from the greenhouse and make a casserole to add to the evening meal. She thought they wouldn't enjoy it, but I convinced her we had nothing to lose. Well, the casserole was a huge hit with everyone, including the cousins in the kitchen. They were going to send a casserole to Steven and Sean at Wisteria. Elizabeth wanted directions, telling Madeleine that Thomas told her it was a better breakfast food than the gruel they had been giving the twins.

Thomas and Elizabeth loved their new home in town. It was indeed very large, and had tall trees in the back yard that would support a great tree house. They offered to babysit for Mary-Ann when the time came, but Rebecca was in school now, and the new baby always came to work with her.

Chapter Thirty-One

Country Meadows
Riding Academy Competition

Madeleine's sister came in from Boston and was given the cabin next to Madeleine's. Elizabeth's parents flew in. Instead of staying with their daughter, they settled in one of the large A-frames for a week's holiday, giving their daughter and family some space.

Some of the visitors flew their horses into the airport, and were met with horse trailers driven by Sandra and her cousins, transporting them to the ranch barns. Friends from other locations in the U.S. drove in, turning onto the newly constructed roads crossing the ranchland, stabling their horses at the barns, and continuing onto their accommodations at the A-frames.

The cousins closed the ranch kitchen and served cafeteria style at the cabin site. The structure was a very large A-frame with a kitchen on one side and tables on the other. The guests could eat in or take their meals to the gazebos.

On the day of the event, the Formidable Seven, dressed in exquisite frilly dresses, extravagant hats and elaborate hair-dos, met guests at the entrances to the cabins and the town. Bands welcomed them at both entrances, and another band marched the perimeter of the show jumping ring, entertaining people as they chose their seats in the grandstands. They were given stemmed glasses and champagne, later being offered refills of wine. Finger foods were delivered throughout the event.

Richard and Madeleine took turns announcing the events and riders. She had the teens begin the competition, followed in the afternoon by the ladies' class. The next day began with the children, followed in the afternoon by the men's class.

The grounds and the grandstand were a sea of colorful hats, gowns, and men's fancy dress. Many wore morning suits which you can be sure were purchased especially for this affair.

As it was an informal competition, cash prizes were not awarded, but horses were adorned with fancy ribbons, given in the winner's circle after each event. Ty and his team were in attendance, their function to adjust jumps and rearrange the course when required. They worked tirelessly and had a lot of fun. What a change from their missions!

On the second day, Rebecca started the children's class. She and her horse looked like a seasoned team, meeting each challenge with such grace that it took my breath away. There was a wide slope between the sidewalks and riding ring, protecting the competitors from distractions from the guests, especially with those fancy hats, bobbing about the grounds. Madeleine made an announcement before each competition, asking visitors to be mindful of making any noise close to the ring, and there was a notice at the top of the programs as well.

However there's always one in every crowd. A lady from the town, known to draw attention to herself wore a particularly large hat, and was walking on the sidewalk close to the corner jump as Rebecca was approaching in deep concentration. The lady let out a horrible screeching laugh and threw one arm in the air. Rebecca's horse spooked, taking off on a full gallop, nostrils flared and eyes wild with fear. Rebecca was afraid it would run right into the fence, but talked softly, reining it to the left, keeping it within the ring. When she came close to the third corner, still out of control, the gate opened wide behind her and Sandra shot in like a bullet. She glided up beside Rebecca's horse, guiding her horse to cover the view of the frightened run-away, slowing it down and calming it. Richard hopped the fence and grabbed Rebecca as Sandra reached over and slipped her to the ground.

Once the danger was over, I looked around to see Will guiding the obnoxious lady through the far gate into the town. She wouldn't calm down, so he locked her in the small jail cell, and sat with her until she became more manageable. He observed her many times in the boardroom. He had a suspicion that it had something to do with food allergies or medication. With her consent, he called the

181

doctor in and discussed it with him. Eventually the lady agreed to blood tests and listened to the advice she was given. Within the next few weeks, the treatment worked and she became a different person. She brought Will a huge bouquet of flowers, and thanked him for his concern and astute insight.

Back to the competition, Rebecca brought up the end of the children's event on Sandra's horse. Everyone was very quiet, watching this small, brave competitor on this very tall horse. Sandra hung on the edge of the fence, tense, but proud. On Rebecca's insistence, they made the jumps taller, appropriate for a horse of this category. When she entered the winner's circle, the crowd all gave her a standing ovation honoring her for her advanced skills as a rider.

Between each event, the choir took the stage at the side of the ring, entertaining the guests, as the new jumps were set up for the next event. At the end of the second day, they put on a musical, followed by fireworks set up and supervised by Ty's team – an awesome end to a classy competition.

Chapter Thirty-Two

Sanja Plans the Future

Ty told me that the team was taking a few months off, giving the younger team a chance to take on any missions required of them. They were already three months into their time, first completing a few projects before returning to the ranch.

The men would be staying part of the time at the house, but for the most part at the A-frame 'village' next to the stables. After their experience at the 'competition', a few of them gained interest in learning to jump horses. They offered to help maintain the academy, as well as build a greenhouse near Harry's farm.

Ty would live at the house. He planned to run every morning with Sandra and Richard; afterwards taking in the first round of golf with Anthony. He would spend some time helping Papa maintain the golf course. The rest of his time would be spent on surveillance, and planning operations with the other team Captain. The 'Glowsticks' would spell off the other shooters, as the burnout on that particular position is high.

A couple of weeks after the competition, Sanja came upstairs from his room on the lower floor, poured two Blue Martinis, placing them on the table on the balcony, then instructed Robert to rouse me from bed.

After showering, I came out to the balcony to join him.

He asked if I had thought about paying my Canadian friends a visit. I always had the Canadian Registry open on the corner of the kitchen counter, calling one of my friends every morning for a chat as I shared my morning Blue Martini with Freddie. I noticed the pages were often opened to different sections I had marked for easy access to phone numbers. I asked if he was looking through the book, and he replied affirmative.

Answering his question, "I'm not so sure that it would be wise to leave the security of my home, and I couldn't even consider leaving Robert, Freddie and Benjamin for a very long period of time. There are my garden parties on Fridays and golfing every Monday with 'the ladies'."

Sanja told me he had been working on something for months. He noted the location of each of my family and friends, scouted out private air strips within fairly close proximity to each, then flew to each location, searching for suitable accommodations nearby, such as cabanas, beach houses, or small villas. One stipulation was that the places had to be animal friendly. Where possible, he purchased a summer home or cabin, and the team over the past three months were repairing and updating the structures. He found a particularly charming villa in Mexico not far from my brother's place. My brother agreed to keep an eye on it in exchange for the use for the occasional guest. Ty and his team had contacts all over the world, and were very helpful in the matter of locating suitable accommodations. Those were the projects Ty had been referring to earlier.

I told him I thought it was very hard to transport animals. Shipping them by airlines was a traumatic experience.

He said "I have been training Robert, Benjamin and Freddie to take trips. I load them into the small back seat of the sports car, drive into the cavity of the plane, settle them into a large doggie bed, and take off for a flight. They love it. I'm surprised you didn't notice them gone."

I took a few minutes to absorb the information, then answered "It's not unusual for them to hang out at the stables, or at Thomas and Elizabeth's for long periods of time, so I notice when they're gone, but I don't worry."

I went on "I've seen them in the sports car, which by the way, is a very comical spectacle. You would be gone for a long period, but I thought you just had them at the lake for the day. They often returned with sand in their fur. It didn't occur to me to question you, as I knew they would be always kept safe. They'd come home so excited, having enjoyed their day with you."

Sanja answered "It was hard for your brother to keep a secret all this time, but I took the three with me to Mexico, checking on the repairs and upgrades that Ty and his team were making to the villa. They know your brother and his wife, and have fun catching sticks and chasing gulls."

I shook my head "I just can't believe what I'm hearing. Here I am holding garden parties, while you're off with 'the babies' meeting people and buying villas."

He smiled "It started me thinking when I spent that weekend at the lake with you. I realized there was so much more to life. I have no regrets for the time I've spent poking around in brains, or assisting on missions, but it was time for a complete change, and one that involved you. I started looking for a plane, got very excited over the jet complete with sports car, and the rest is history."

He asked "So how about some adventure?" The "three babies" were at our feet by this time, sensing plans that included them.

The following week, I packed a medium sized suitcase with some versatile clothing, and arranged with Mary-Ann to ship another suitcase to 'the next destination' when I needed a new wardrobe. Mary-Ann and Alicia were pleased to take over garden parties for a period unknown. I was ready to go. The family had a big bon voyage party at Wisteria on Sunday night.

186

Monday morning at four a.m., we loaded our three fuzzy friends and two pieces of luggage into the tiny sports car, and drove to the airstrip before daybreak.

Sanja took off down the runway and headed for the clouds. He made a full circle around the ranch, town, and hotel, then flew off into the morning sunrise.

THE END

Made in the USA
Charleston, SC
24 October 2012